Mañanaland

PAM MUÑOZ RYAN

SCHOLASTIC PRESS

land

NEW YORK

All rights reserved. Published by Scholastic Press, an imprint of Scholastic Inc.,
Publishers since 1920. SCHOLASTIC, SCHOLASTIC PRESS, and associated logos are
trademarks and/or registered trademarks of Scholastic Inc.

The publisher does not have any control over and does not assume any
responsibility for author or third-party websites or their content.

This book is a work of fiction. Names, characters, places, and incidents
are either the product of the author's imagination or are used fictitiously,
and any resemblance to actual persons, living or dead, business establishments,
events, or locales is entirely coincidental.

Library of Congress Cataloging-in-Publication Data Available

ISBN 978-1-338-15786-4

10 9 8 7 6 5 4 3 2 1   20 21 22 23 24

Printed in the U.S.A.   23
First edition, March 2020

To my mother,
Esperanza "Hope" Muñoz Bell,
for protecting me
beyond measure.

YESTERDAY

One

Somewhere in the Américas, many years after once-upon-a-time and long before happily-ever-after, a boy climbed the cobbled steps of an arched bridge in the tiny village of Santa Maria, in the country of the same name.

He bounced a fútbol on each stone ledge.

In the land of a hundred bridges, this was his favorite. When he was only a baby, Papá, a master stonemason and bridge builder, had carved his name on the spandrel wall for all to see.

MAXIMILIANO CÓRDOBA

On his bridge, Max liked the going up of it.

He liked that when he reached the threshold, the deck breached Río Bobinado in a long bumpy alley. He dropped the ball and dribbled it toward the middle of the deck, bouncing it off the sides of his dusty huarache sandals.

Here above the keystone, he could see all of his world before him and the river below, curving away from Santa Maria, looping back and curving away again. He moved his hand to mimic the river's erratic path as it circled the islets and giant boulders. Why was Río Bobinado so indecisive?

Max glanced over his shoulder to make sure Papá hadn't caught up. "Once . . ." he whispered, ". . . a gargantuan serpent as wide as twenty houses and as long as three states could not decide whether to slither west toward the ocean or east toward the mountains. As soon as the serpent chose one direction, the other seemed far more appealing. Back and forth it went, side-winding across the earth, its body leaving a huge chasm in its wake. The chasm eventually filled with rain and became the river."

Satisfied, Max smiled. This was his favorite spot to make up stories and wonder about big and bewildering things: How long it would take to grow up and become a man, if he would ever see what lay beyond the horizon, and why his mother left and whether he'd ever meet her.

Max knew that Papá didn't like big questions of any kind, especially ones about the past or the future. Some of them even seemed to cause him pain. Max couldn't count the times Papá had instructed him to "stand firmly in the reality of today or life will only disappoint you tomorrow."

He pushed Papá's words aside and gazed out at the village. The more prominent houses—greens, yellows, blues—hugged the riverbanks. The spire of the chapel, Our Lady of Sorrows, pointed toward the heavens. Citrus orchards and grape fields bordered the outskirts of town. Nestled in the foothills on dirt roads, modest white stone cottages perched like patient doves at roost. Max shaded his eyes until he spotted his. Was Buelo already cooking dinner with Lola at his side, begging for scraps?

He let his gaze continue upward toward a jagged cliff where a stone tower loomed. Everyone called the stronghold La Reina Gigante, the giant queen, because she looked like the most powerful piece on a chessboard. Max loved that wherever he went in Santa Maria, he could see at least the merlons and crenels of her crown, as if she was always watching over him. He even had a faint memory of sitting at her feet while red blossoms rained upon him. Had it been a dream?

The palace surrounding La Reina Gigante had once been majestic, too. But that was decades before the cannons of ancient armies demolished the roof, an earthquake unsteadied the walls, and a war in the neighboring country of Abismo forced legions of people to flee a dictator, using the ruins as a safe place to hide. Some said these "hidden ones" were poor innocents—women and children. Others said they were malicious criminals, filthy beggars, and the unwanted.

No one had ever seen a hidden one to know for sure. But it was rumored that their spirits returned each year on the wings of the peregrine falcon.

Sometimes when heavy mist shrouded the hills and Santa Maria fell silent, their ghosts could be heard whispering prayers to the giant queen for her protection and guidance, as if she was a saint or a guardian angel. *Everyone* knew someone who knew someone who had heard them.

The entire property around La Reina Gigante and the ruins was fenced, abandoned, and off-limits. Only Papá had permission from the mayor to commandeer the rubble to build new bridges. For as long as he could remember, Max had begged Papá to take him to see La Reina and the ruins up close. He'd be a hero among his friends if he was the first boy to cross the haunted gates! Just because Papá didn't believe in ghosts didn't mean they weren't there. Maybe this summer Papá would finally take him. He *was* almost twelve.

Max leaned over the capstones, warm from the afternoon sun, and waited for Papá to catch up. In the river, he saw half of his head reflected: a mop of black curls, heavy eyebrows, and caramel-colored eyes. Buelo called them tiger eyes and said they were a sign of strength and determination. Chuy called them leche quemada eyes, like their favorite milk and brown sugar candy. Some of the boys at school called them devil eyes. Max did his best to ignore them. But he wondered if the boys knew something about him that he did not. Was he filled with badness? Still, they were his mother's eyes and one of the few things about her he could claim. That, and a tiny silver compass on a leather cord that once belonged to her. He patted his chest and felt it beneath his shirt.

As he tossed a pebble into the river, he let the rippling water turn his heavy thoughts to happier ones. School was out, and tryouts for the village fútbol team were in five weeks. Like all his closest friends, he dreamed of making the team.

Max picked up the ball and threw it at the parapet, letting it ricochet back so he could catch it. The bumpy stones sent the ball in unpredictable directions, forcing Max to hover and anticipate. He kicked it hard, and when it hit the wall and flew back at him, he batted it down.

"Bravo!" Papá yelled. "Don't unsettle any of the facing though. Or I'll have repairs." His cheeks flushed with ruddy circles and his forehead wrinkled from his usual troubled frown.

"You know I can't kick as hard as you," said Max. Papá was broad shouldered and solid, a wall of strength and muscle. He and Buelo had both played goalie on Santa Maria's national team, and Max wanted to one day do the same. He was already as tall as both of them, but scrawny.

Max kicked the ball up and caught it in his hands. "Do you remember that tryouts are next month?"

"It's hard to forget when you remind me so often." Papá almost smiled.

"I was wondering . . . My fútbol shoes are *nearly* too small and the toes will need wrapping soon. If I had a pair of Volantes, the ones with the fancy wings on the side, I'd *surely* make the team." He looked at Papá hopefully.

"Your shoes are fine for now. And expensive ones that we can't afford won't make you a better player. A world of disappointment comes from wishing for what you cannot—"

Before Papá could finish, a falcon swooped overhead, low enough that both he and Max ducked. Its sickle-shaped wings were splayed and taut. The head and hooked bill stretched forward, baring a white neck and speckled breast. They shaded their eyes, mesmerized by the silent flight.

"It's so big," said Max as it caught a current and soared away.

"Peregrine," said Papá. "A female that has come back to nest."

Whose spirit did it bring on its wing? wondered Max. "They say—" he started, then thought better of repeating the superstition. "They say they come back to the same spot every year."

Papá nodded. "It's true. But I haven't seen one

that large for a long time, and it is a little late to nest. Others have already come and gone." He put an arm around Max's shoulder and hugged him to his side. "Let's go, slowpoke."

"Me? Slow?" Max quickly dribbled the fútbol across the deck and called over his shoulder, "I'm going to meet Chuy at the field, and I'll *still* beat you home because you have to stop and talk to everyone!"

"Come home right after. Buelo went fishing this morning and dinner will be ready in an hour or so. I don't want to have to come looking."

"Okay!" Max yelled back. Papá had only recently allowed him to go to the field on his own. Max didn't want to give him a reason to take back the small freedom, or upset him. Saturday was Papá's night out with his friends and Max's night in with Buelo, and he wanted to keep it that way.

By the time Max reached the bridge's landing, he felt as free as the soaring peregrine. Summer was the infinite sky before him. He had months to swim in the water hole, play fútbol with his friends, and get ready for tryouts. Tonight, he would go to sleep with a belly full of fish after an evening of trading stories with Buelo—fantastical tales about dragons and serpents, or river monsters and trolls . . .

He clutched the ball to his chest and jumped toward the bank, taking two steps at a time.

On his bridge, he even liked the going down of it.

Two

The field was more of a bald spot than a grassy park but good enough for practice or a pickup game. Real games were held at the secondary school a few miles away.

A group of boys warmed up, juggling balls knee to knee or passing to one another. Now that Max and most of his friends were turning twelve, they could finally try out for the village team. Santa Maria was crazy for fútbol, and the local team had won the last two regional championships. People flooded to their games. This year, the league was sending a new coach to Santa Maria. All eyes would be on him and his players.

Chuy waved Max onto the field.

"Your hair! What happened?" said Max. Yesterday Chuy had a mop of curls like Max. Now it was buzzed close to his scalp.

"It was so long, my sisters were trying to braid it."

Max laughed. He could picture the three little girls doing that. Even though they could be annoying, and Chuy complained about them all the time, Max would have loved a baby sister or brother to whom he could tell stories, give piggyback rides, and share secrets.

Chuy ran a hand over his shorn head. "Besides, I don't want anyone to confuse you and me."

"That will never happen!" said Max. Chuy had a broad chest and was solid to the core, an avocado straight from the tree. Max was a pointy blade of agave.

"Come on." He herded Max to the field where Ortiz and Guillermo were kicking balls back and forth.

"Max!" called Ortiz. "Come to pay your respects to Ortiz the Great?" He liked to remind the boys that he was the son of a councilman, lived in the biggest house in all of Santa Maria, and was older by almost a year. His voice had recently changed and sounded like a man's. He was a head taller than the rest, with thick muscular thighs. And there were wisps of hair already growing above his lip.

"The great *what*?" said Max. "Fanfarrón?"

All the boys laughed because it was true. He was a braggart.

Ortiz shrugged. "If you are the best, you should tell the world." He shook a finger at Max. "You'll see. Let's play."

Chuy held up his hands to make an announcement. "Okay, everyone! Ortiz and Max are goalies. My talent on the field is up for grabs!"

The boys jeered and quickly sorted teams.

Max and Ortiz went to opposite ends of the field where makeshift goalie cages had been hammered together from wood scraps. Someone placed a ball midfield and took the kickoff. The boys ran hard, some barefooted, some in ratty shoes with no laces, some in huaraches, like Max, saving their fútbol shoes for the real games during the season. Max protected almost every shot on goal. Ortiz missed many of his, but when he did get the ball, his throws and kicks were long and hard.

They played until the sun was low. Then Max, Ortiz, Gui, and Chuy huddled around an old water spigot sticking up from the ground and gulped long drinks. As they headed back toward the bridge together, Ortiz announced, "I have news. My father talked to—"

"Shush . . ." hissed Gui, spreading his arms out to stop them. He pointed to a tree arching over the road. "Look."

The falcon sat on a branch, chest puffed, preening its feathers.

Max kept his voice low. "Female peregrine. I saw it earlier."

The bird leaned forward.

"She's watching us," whispered Chuy.

"She's huge," whispered Ortiz.

Max nudged him. "Don't worry. She only eats pigeons." As they inched closer, the falcon opened her wings and lifted in a languid, elegant arc, her yellow legs like two spent arrows tucked tightly beneath a fanned tail. She sailed toward La Reina Gigante.

In a somber voice, Gui said, "She has brought the ghosts of the hidden ones. That's what my brother says."

Ortiz smirked. "You'll believe anything."

Gui shook his head. "There *were* hidden ones. Guardians helped them run away from Abismo. Their spirits return on the wings of the peregrine."

Max grinned, recalling how he and Chuy used to put on capes and masks and pretend to be Los Guardianes de los Escondidos, the Guardians of the Hidden Ones. He picked up a stick, raised his arm as if holding a sword, and lunged forward. "Gui's right. The hidden ones fled Abismo because of a cruel dictator. The guardians bravely guided them through Santa Maria to safety."

Chuy picked up a stick, too, and fenced with an imaginary attacker. "The guardians wore disguises and were invincible. No matter the danger, they carried on to help those in need."

"Stop!" said Ortiz. "You're both acting like you're five years old. Want to know the real truth?"

"That is the truth," said Max.

Ortiz shook his head. "My parents said the hidden ones were dangerous—murderers and thieves—the worst of the worst. Why do you think they were cast out of their own country? You don't see any of them living in Santa Maria, do you? That's because if they'd shown their faces, they would have been driven out of town."

Chuy shook his head. "But the guardians—"

"—were criminals, too," said Ortiz. "They broke the law by protecting the hidden ones. If they'd been caught, they would have been arrested and thrown in jail. But what does it matter? That's ancient history. Does anyone want to hear *my* news? About the new coach?"

Max and Chuy tossed their sticks aside and crowded close to hear.

"Okay, okay," said Ortiz. "My father talked to my cousin who manages the fútbol clinics in Santa Inés and has friends in the league. Our new coach is Héctor Cruz."

Gui held up a finger. "Héctor Cruz? He's great! When he played pro, he broke the national record for most goals in a championship game." Gui may have been the youngest and smallest of all the boys, barely old enough to try out for the team this year, but he knew fútbol on and off the field.

"Let me finish," said Ortiz. "He has lots of contacts with the higher-level teams so he's a good one to impress. My cousin said Coach Cruz is strict about the league rules. Just to register for tryouts, everybody has to be the right age and prove residence."

"What does that mean?" asked Max.

"Your address has to be in Santa Maria, and at least one parent has to live with you," said Ortiz. "So kids from other towns can't take spots from us. And you have to prove your birthday so no one older can play in our league. Otherwise it's not fair."

"Remember when we played the team from Valencia?" said Gui. "Everyone *knew* the center forward wasn't eleven!"

"He looked like he was old enough to drive!" said Max.

Chuy laughed. "Or get married."

"But how do we prove it?" asked Max.

"Birth certificates," said Ortiz. "Of course, then you have to make the team. And the competition will be tough."

They all nodded.

"Anyone up for practicing tomorrow?" asked Chuy. "Max, maybe your father can come and give us some pointers."

Before Max could agree, Ortiz threw up his arms. "Are you going to let me finish? I was going to tell you that my cousin has empty spots in one of his summer clinics. He said I could come and bring some friends. No tuition either. We would take the bus to Santa Inés every day during the week until tryouts. Are you guys in?"

Max's and Chuy's mouths fell open. The clinics had the reputation of being skill builders—drills and scrimmages under the watchful eye of coaches all day, five days a week. Players couldn't help but have an advantage at the tryouts.

"I know I can convince my parents," said Gui. "I'm definitely in."

"Me too," Chuy echoed.

"I'd give *anything* to do that," said Max. "I'll ask when I get home." He hoped he could convince Papá, who found a reason to say no to everything.

"I'm going to Santa Inés tomorrow and staying the night with my cousin before the first day of the clinic. Héctor Cruz is coming for dinner." Ortiz strutted. "Always good to know the coach personally, right? Otherwise, I'd ride up with you commoners on the bus Monday morning."

Chuy rolled his eyes at Max.

Ortiz dropped his ball and dribbled forward. His footwork was quick. He spun around and headed back toward them, catching the ball with his toe and popping it up into his hands. "Just call me Nandito, the greatest footballer ever." He bowed.

Max laughed. "Ortiz, you better hurry if you want to catch up to him. He played for the professional club, Los Lobos, when he was only fourteen. And the national team when he was eighteen."

"Your grandfather played against him at El Coliseo, the giant stadium!" said Gui.

"Right. In a tournament game," said Max. Buelo still carried the worn photo in his wallet of him and the phenomenal young footballer, Nandito, with their arms around each other.

"And your father played on the national team, too. He still holds two unbroken records," said Gui. "One for most saved goals in a season and one for most saved goals in tournament play."

"Fútbol is in your blood," said Chuy.

Max hoped it was true. And that the talent hadn't skipped him. If he made the village team and they won the championship again, he'd get his name and photo in all the newspapers. People would recognize him. Maybe even his mother.

"How come you don't look like your father or grandfather?" asked Ortiz. "You're so tall and skinny. Maybe you should play basketball instead."

"Don't listen to him," said Chuy. "You've got talent running through your veins. He just doesn't want the competition."

"Your father only played professional for one year though," said Gui. "Was he injured? I couldn't find any record that he was released."

Max hesitated. "He never talks about it."

"My mom said he *quit* the team because he met your mother. Then she left him," said Ortiz. "Some love story, huh?"

Max felt a jab in his heart. Everyone usually tiptoed around the subject of his mother.

Chuy raised both hands and made a sound of disgust. "Ortiz, what's the matter with you? Your mother talks too much and so do you!"

"What? *Everybody* knows she disappeared. Anyway, who *leaves* the national team?" Ortiz began dribbling the ball from one side of the road to the other and back toward them. "But your grandfather played with Nandito! Not everyone can say that. I have a prediction. Someday *I'll* make the national team, and you three will say *you* played fútbol with *me*."

"Or you'll be telling people *you* played with *us*," said Chuy.

"Not likely," said Ortiz, laughing and running ahead.

Chuy slung an arm around Max's shoulder. "Tomorrow at one o'clock? We can practice and make plans for the bus ride to Santa Inés on Monday."

Gui nudged Max. "Aren't you excited?"

Max nodded and grinned. He was. And relieved that they had stepped away from talk of his mother. Any mention of her always surprised him, like the little toy he once had, la caja sorpresa—a box he cranked until a clown on a spring popped up when he least expected it—taunting him with buried questions.

Three

Max dribbled the fútbol along the dusty path to the cottage, remembering the first time la caja sorpresa had burst open.

He was in grade two, playing marbles in the dirt on the playground with a new boy after school. All the other children had already gone home. A teacher sat nearby, waiting with them.

"My mamá is always late," said the boy. "Where's yours?"

Max frowned. "She lives far away."

"Where?"

Max shrugged. Why hadn't Papá told him?

The boy laughed. "You don't know where your own mother lives?"

The teacher jumped up, quickly pulled the boy aside, and whispered something to him.

Solemnly, the boy nodded, then returned to the marble game.

"What did she say?" Max whispered.

"That you're a poor motherless child and it's not polite to talk about her."

"How come?" asked Max. Other kids had parents who didn't live with them.

The boy shrugged. "She said it might make you feel sad and unworthy. Want to play tag?"

As they began chasing each other, Max thought about what the boy had said. It wasn't *sadness* he felt. It was a peculiar *nothingness* tucked behind a veil of secrecy that no one was willing to lift. Not Papá. Not Buelo. Not his neighbors or teachers. What did they know that he didn't? He ran after the boy and the words echoed . . . *poor* . . . *motherless* . . . *unworthy* . . .

Later, as he'd walked home with Buelo and Papá, he asked, "Why did my mother leave? Where did she go? When is she coming back?"

Papá looked startled. "Max, where is this coming from?"

Max repeated what the boy had said.

Papá stopped and knelt in front of him, his eyes

desperate. "Please understand. I don't have all the answers. I don't know where she is, and I don't know if she's ever coming back."

"Have you looked for her?"

"Of course. I've never *stopped* looking," said Papá.

"So you can ask her to come home and we can be a family?"

Papá sighed. "When you're older, I'll explain more. But now, you and me and Buelo . . ." He put his hand over his heart. ". . . *we* are a family." He stood and walked on.

Buelo took Max's hand. "This is a very painful subject for your father. Can you see that?"

Max nodded. His eyes brimmed. "But I don't know anything about her. I don't remember . . ."

"How could you? You were not even a year old when she left," said Buelo. "Your father will share more when you are both ready. I will talk to him. Would you like that?"

Max nodded as tears rolled down his face.

"Did . . . did . . . she leave because of me? Because I was unworthy?"

Buelo pulled Max close and wiped his cheeks with his handkerchief. "Unworthy? No. You have never given anyone a reason to leave. The only thing you have ever given this family is joy. If your mother could see the fine boy you are, she'd be proud."

Max leaned into Buelo's chest. "Will I ever meet her?"

"Solo mañana sabe. Only the place we know as tomorrow holds the answers."

It wasn't much comfort. But all the way home Max clung to Buelo's words and whispered, "Solo mañana sabe."

Later, at bedtime, when Papá came into Max's room to say goodnight, he sat on the bed. "I'm sorry I was so abrupt today." He stroked Max's hair. "I know you want to know more about your mother. Her name is Renata Esteban Córdoba. And . . . you have her eyes." He put the leather cord with the compass in Max's hand. "This belonged to her. It had been her mother's. She treasured it and wore it all the time. One day she couldn't find it anywhere and was devastated. After she left, I found it lodged behind a drawer in the dresser. I always hoped to return it to her someday. Until then, I think she would want you to have it."

In the almost dark, Max could see Papá blinking back tears. He didn't want to cause Papá any more pain, so he didn't ask questions. He just hugged his neck.

After Papá left, Max studied the silver compass with its markings for north, south, east, and west. As he turned it, the tiny needle shimmied. Engraved on the back was an elaborate compass rose with eight points of direction. Papá had said he didn't know if she was coming back. Was she waiting to be found? Maybe the compass would guide him toward her, wherever she was, and *Max* could return it. When she met him and realized what a fine boy he was, she might even consider coming home.

Max whispered her name over and over so he

could hear it rolling off his tongue. *"Renata ...*
Renata ... Renata ..."

The nothingness that he had felt for so long had
turned into a little something.

Four

The smell of peppery fish and fresh bread greeted Max before he reached the front gate.

Dinner and excitement about the fútbol clinic overshadowed his thoughts. Still, Max knew he would have to wait for the right moment to ask permission.

Buelo had been busy today. The yard was weeded, the bushes pruned, and the nearby corral for their burro, Dulce, raked. The small stable even had new straw. Max unlatched the front gate and Lola leaped toward him, shimmying and yelping as if it had been days instead of hours since she'd last seen him.

"I missed you, too, girl." Max ruffled the dog's black-and-white head and kissed her giant muzzle. She darted away and returned with a stick in her mouth, nudging his hand. Max tossed it as far as he could, and she ran after it.

Buelo hobbled from the stone cottage. Even with his cane, he liked to say he was as strong as Dulce, just a little slower. His shirtsleeves were rolled up, and a kitchen towel stained from cooking was tucked into the waist of his blue jeans. His wavy white hair seemed to float on his head like a cloud.

"Are you hungry? I caught trucha this morning, your favorite. Junior will be happy, too. Where is he? You beat him home."

Everyone called Papá *Junior* because he was Feliciano Córdoba Jr., after Buelo, who was the first. Max thought the name *Feliciano*, which meant happy, fit Buelo much better than it did Papá. Max's middle name was Feliciano, which seemed right, because he was somewhere between Buelo and Papá on the happiness scale.

"Yes, I'm hungry!" Max's mouth watered at the prospect of fried trout. He followed Buelo inside the stone cottage, which, even during the warmest weather, stayed cool. After Max washed his hands in the sink and set the table, Papá finally walked into the kitchen. He held up a basket covered in a dish towel. "I saw Miss Domínguez."

Max rolled his eyes. "Again? She was my *teacher*. It's embarrassing!"

"It shouldn't bother you. She's not your teacher any longer," said Papá. "And she only told me how much she is going to miss you in her class next year. She said you were very innovative in your approach to solving problems."

Max hid his smile and thought better of telling Papá what she meant. Miss Domínguez had been amused by Max's elaborate explanations for why he was late, or had forgotten his homework, or why he and Chuy should be partners for one project or another. She encouraged his storytelling. Papá, though, would think it immature. "She's being nice because she likes you," said Max.

Papá shook his head. "It's just people helping people. She sees a boy like you and it brings out the mother hen in her. That's all. Some fresh tortillas or bread. A knit hat or sweater. What does it hurt? And

I'm helping to repair her garden wall. Favor con favor se paga."

"A favor for a favor," said Max. "I wish she'd repay you by sending a pair of Volantes in her basket."

Buelo patted Max's shoulder. "Volantes, so your feet can fly. I like your optimism. Now, both of you, sit. Tell me about your day."

"We saw a giant falcon," said Papá. "Female."

"It was gliding in circles." Max waved his arm in the air to demonstrate. "Papá said it was a peregrine. Then I saw it *again* when I was with Chuy, Ortiz, and Gui."

"Twice in one day? Very auspicious," said Buelo. "It's known as the pilgrim bird because it journeys far away to promised lands but always returns to the same area, bringing good fortune and magic. You were lucky to see one."

Papá raised an eyebrow at Buelo then turned to Max. "It's just a myth. It was a coincidence. We happened to be there when it flew over. Only fools believe in luck. Good fortune comes from hard work, careful preparation, and practice."

Max glanced at Buelo and rolled his eyes. Couldn't Papá believe in something as simple as a little good luck?

"I am starting a new footbridge near the outdoor market next week," Papá continued. "That bridge, *not* the falcon, will bring prosperity to the village by making it easier for people to trade and sell."

Buelo grinned. "The new bridge will allow one side of the river to safely hold hands with the other . . ."

Max chimed in, ". . . because a Córdoba bridge never collapses. First things first, then stone by stone. That's how to accomplish anything well."

"That's right," said Papá, nodding proudly.

Papá, Buelo, and his father before him were stonemasons. They kept all the bridges in the land in good repair and built new spans. Already Max knew the best rocks for decking, revetments, and keystones. People often asked him if he was going to follow in his family's footsteps. He never knew quite what to say. Maybe someday, after he became a famous footballer.

But first things first. Max took a deep breath and sat a little straighter. "Papá, tryouts are coming up and . . ." Max cleared his throat. "I need to get in shape and build my strength to be ready." He held up a skinny arm, making a fist to show how much muscle he did *not* have. "Ortiz's cousin is running a summer clinic in Santa Inés and said he can bring some friends. He invited me and Chuy and Gui. We'd take the bus there and back each day. Can I go, Papá?"

Papá didn't even look up from his dinner. "It's too expensive and too far away from home for you to be on your own."

"That's the thing," said Max, leaning forward. "There's *no* tuition! The cousin has extra spots to fill. I wouldn't be alone. I'd be with my friends. You can talk to Ortiz's father about it."

Papá's body tensed. "The answer is no! It does not matter whether it's free or not. It's in a town forty-five minutes away. Anything could happen to you in Santa Inés. And I know Chuy's parents. I can't imagine they will allow him to go either. Besides, Buelo and I can teach you everything you'd learn at the clinic. You have the expertise of two professionals right here in Santa Maria."

"Papá, please . . ." Max begged. He looked to Buelo for help, but he only lowered his eyes. This was Papá's decision. "You *never* let me do anything away from the village! You don't need to worry about me. I'm responsible and I'm not going to disappear like—" Max regretted his words the second he said them.

Papá lay down his fork and stared at his plate. Finally, he looked up and said, "It's others I worry about, Max. And the answer is still no. But . . ." He pointed at him. "You can work for me this summer on the new bridge. I haven't hired an apprentice yet. Then you could earn new fútbol shoes. And lifting stones will build your muscles."

Max slumped in his chair. He could see that Papá wasn't going to change his mind. But if he was right about Chuy's parents, at least Max and Chuy would be together. "Can Chuy be an apprentice, too?"

"If his parents agree," said Papá. "I could use the help. I've already cleared the site. And the foundations and abutments are laid and mortared. I'm going to the ruins on Monday to collect more stones. You two can start unloading them at the bridge site after that."

"Can I go with you to collect the stones?"

"You know the ruins is no place for a boy."

"Papá, I'm almost *twelve*. I'm not little anymore."

"When you're older," said Papá, the tone in his voice saying the subject was closed.

Max didn't press because he knew it was

useless. "We could work until the tryouts. But if we make the team . . ."

"Then I'll hire an apprentice," said Papá.

Buelo raised a finger. "Speaking of that, I heard about the new coach today."

"Me too," said Max. "His name is Héctor Cruz and he's really strict about the rules. We have to prove our age and where we live just to register for tryouts. Everyone needs their birth certificate."

"Our team has always respected the rules," said Buelo.

Max continued. "But some teams didn't and some boys were older than they were supposed to be. I wish Ortiz was too old to play. He's trying out for goalie, too. He's a lot bigger than me and has a mustache!"

"Bigger doesn't mean better," said Buelo. "Quickness counts."

"Today I saved more shots on goal than he did," said Max.

"See," said Buelo.

"But he was better at throwing and kicking."

"Max, you are skilled at forward, too, not just at goalie," said Papá. "And keep in mind that not everyone makes the village team the first year they try out. It's better not to get your hopes up. Besides, you're still pretty young to be on a team that travels around the state. I'm not sure how I feel about that."

"*You* played on the village team when you were my age."

"That was different."

Max felt heat rise to his face. Different how? Why couldn't Papá have faith that Max could look out for himself? Why couldn't Papá be *a little* optimistic? "I want to make it this year! And play goalie like you and Buelo. If I make it, one of you would come to every game anyway."

Buelo muttered, "He's persistent, Junior, like someone else I know."

Papá sighed. "True enough."

"Can you start training me and Chuy tomorrow?"

Papá nodded. "As long as we get home by three

o'clock. Your aunties and uncle are coming for dinner. And your uncle and I are going to play a little chess. It's time I won a game from Mayor Rodrigo Soto."

Max smiled. His aunties were really his great aunts—Buelo's sisters, Amelia and Mariana. Amelia was married to Tío Rodrigo, the mayor of Santa Maria.

"Plus, you need to give Lola a bath tomorrow afternoon." Papá pushed up from the table. "I won't be late tonight." He pointed to Buelo. "Don't fill his mind with nonsense."

"Stay out as long as you like," said Buelo.

Before he left, Papá kissed Max on the head. "Go to bed when Buelo says."

Max nodded, stealing a look at Buelo, who winked at him.

Five

Buelo and Max made themselves comfortable in their usual places—Max on the sofa and Buelo with a cup of coffee in the overstuffed chair that sagged in all the right places.

Lola walked in circles and finally lay on the tiles in front of the fireplace. This time of year the fire-box was cold, and the grate cradled only brooms of herbs that Buelo had collected. Max caught a whiff of dried rosemary, which always made him think of summertime and storytelling.

"You first," said Buelo.

"Today I was wondering about Río Bobinado." Max told him his story about the gargantuan serpent with the indecisive spirit creating the chasm that became the coiling river.

Buelo nodded. "A serpent that could not make up its mind. Perhaps that is why anyone who travels the river's path is plagued with uncertainty and apprehension."

"Is that true?"

Buelo smiled. "It could be. We all face something in life that is a mystery, where no matter which way we look, there is no satisfying answer." Buelo shrugged. "But such is the challenge of life. Your story reminds us of that."

Max put his hands behind his head, letting the idea settle. He liked that his story could have a double meaning, and one he'd never even considered. Miss Domínguez said that a good story left you wondering. The next time he saw her, if Papá wasn't around, he would tell her this one.

Buelo held up a finger. "My turn. How about 'The Secret Bridge and the Guardabarrera'? I'll need a little help in the telling. Remind me, how do I begin?"

Max smiled. "*You* know. Once upon a time . . ." he prompted.

Buelo cleared his throat. "Once upon a time, a

grandfather told his grandson a true story . . ."

Max giggled. "You say that every time."

Buelo swept an arm toward the window and cleared his throat. "Once upon a time in the north, far away and hidden, there was a secret bridge, which was only discussed in whispers among bridge builders, their descendants, and chosen ones." He held a finger to his lips. "In fact, it still exists so you must promise never to tell anyone about it."

"I promise, Buelo."

"Before you reach the secret bridge, you must first cross a glorious span with three arches. It glows pink in the morning sun—the Bridge of a Thousand Mallards."

"Which makes for a lot of quacking," added Max.

"To be sure," said Buelo. "After you cross the bridge to river left . . . Do you remember what that is?"

Max nodded. "If I'm looking downstream, the bank on my left."

"Very good. After you cross to river left, you follow the bank north for another hour until the channel grows weary of all its meanderings and loosens into a long ribbon, becoming deep and calm. It is *there* that you will come upon—"

"—what looks like a dead-end cove, but it's an inlet that leads to a hidden arm of the river," said Max. "That's where the secret bridge is."

"Who is telling the story?" said Buelo. "But you are right. At the back of what looks like a cove is a bridge that is so overgrown with vines and shrubs that it creates a wall of greenery, obscuring anything on the other side. There, a peculiar gatekeeper, a guardabarrera, lives beneath the bridge. *She* determines who may travel beyond. And because she lives in a cavern, some say she is—"

"—a troll with gray skin and yellow eyes, warts, and a nose too big for her face. Or a river witch," said Max. "Is she?"

Buelo smiled. "I will only confirm that she is a creature of great wisdom and intrigue with a mesmerizing aura. She is a keeper of lost things. A collector of sorts. Her cavern is crowded from ceiling to sod. There, you might come to retrieve what you have lost, or deliver something you have found that someone might come looking for one day."

"Like what?"

"Perhaps you lost something of deep meaning when you were on a picnic on the riverbank, a piece of jewelry or something of sentimental value. Or maybe you've lost your way in life. Or cannot find the answers to perplexing questions. She can help."

Max wondered if the guardabarrera knew where his mother was. And if she could help find her so that Max could return the compass. Papá had said that she treasured it. He clutched the compass, rubbing the smooth glass with his thumb.

"But sadly, very few are willing to travel and meet her face-to-face."

"Because they are afraid of what she might be," said Max.

"Yes. But the strong and determined, such as yourself, will find her."

Max smiled and sat a little straighter. He was

glad Buelo presumed such a thing, even if it was only in a made-up story.

"When you reach the cavern door, you must knock four times. She will call out, 'Who stands before me?' And you answer . . ."

"A pilgrim, true of heart," said Max.

"And when she opens the door, you will introduce yourself."

"I am Maximiliano Feliciano Esteban Córdoba, son of Feliciano Córdoba Jr. and grandson of Feliciano Córdoba Sr."

"And she will say . . ." prompted Buelo.

"'I am Yadra, nothing more, nothing less.'"

Buelo nodded. "If you are very fortunate and are indeed true of heart, she may invite you on a journey upriver where you might . . ." He cupped his fingers.

". . . hold tomorrow in the palm of my hand. But how will that help me?" asked Max.

"Oh, so much might be realized by glimpsing what is yet to come. Wouldn't you want to know if the path you are on is leading to a place you want to go? The knowledge might inspire you to change how you live today. Wouldn't you like answers to questions that puzzle you?"

Max nodded. He would like to know if he'd make the fútbol team and where his mother was and if she was ever coming home. He sat up. "You've met the guardabarrera, Buelo, right?"

"Many times, though it has been quite a few years now. Once, we even had tea, which she served in a china cup. And I went on the journey."

"You held tomorrow?" whispered Max. "What did it feel like?"

"I suppose it might be different for everyone. For me, one moment it was warm and syrupy, like a cinnamon pastel just from the oven. And the next, cool and smooth, like a rock pulled from the riverbed. Mostly, though, tomorrow was very slippery. As soon as I thought I'd captured it, *swoosh*, it slid through my fingers and was gone."

"Was your path leading to the place you wanted to go?"

Buelo nodded. "Oh, yes."

"How did you know where the bridge was?" asked Max.

Buelo held up a finger, his eyes twinkling. "A map, of course."

"Can I see it?"

"All in good time, Maximiliano. But remember, your father would remind us, it is just a story. Then again, he is not here." He smiled.

Buelo wanted him to believe, whether there was a map or not.

The clock in the kitchen ticked. Lola snored. Buelo slurped a long sip of coffee.

"Buelo, why is Papá so serious? He always thinks the worst is going to happen."

"Your Papá was once quite lighthearted," said Buelo. "But now he wears his worries and fears like a cloak. The grown-up world robbed him of a bit of his spirit, and he lost his belief in happy endings."

"You mean . . . when my mother left?"

Buelo nodded.

"She stole a piece of his spirit?" asked Max.

"You could say that."

"Didn't he look for her?"

"He looks for her everywhere he goes."

Max thought of the bridges his father had built all over the country. Were those jobs—that sometimes kept him away for weeks at a time—just excuses to look for her?

"Maybe the guardabarrera could help him find her."

Buelo sighed. "Yes, well . . . she would have to *want* to be found." He stood and patted Max's legs. "That is enough for tonight. It is past your bedtime and I need to take Lola out. Now, promise me that when you grow up and meet the guardabarrera, you will tell her hello for me."

Max smiled and went along with Buelo's fantasy. "I promise."

"Good night, Maximiliano. Te quiero."

Max's heart swelled. "Good night, Buelo. I love you, too."

Before he climbed into bed, he stood in front of the small window in his room and looked up. The world was moonlit and on the distant cliff top, La Reina Gigante glowed, diminutive and delicate, as if he could reach out and hold her in his hand. Fog wrapped the tower's waist. A trailing mist drifted at her sides. She was a guardian angel with out-stretched arms.

Max slipped the leather cord with the compass off his neck and carefully set it on the windowsill. Then, like the hidden ones, he prayed to the giant queen for protection and guidance. "La Reina, please watch over Papá, Buelo, my aunties and uncle, Lola, and me. Can you please watch over my mother, too, wherever she is?"

Six

Sunday afternoon, Max left ahead of Papá to meet Chuy at the field.

He stopped at the store to buy two pieces of leche quemada, which he shoved in the pocket of his shorts for later when he and Chuy could celebrate their new summer jobs.

"Max!" Chuy jogged toward him. "What did your father say?"

"Probably the same as your parents. No. But he said you and I could be his apprentices this summer. He'll pay us!" Max laid out the plan of working on weekdays and going to the secret water hole on weekends.

Chuy hung his head and stared at the ground.

"What's wrong?" asked Max.

"I'm *going* to the clinic."

"Your parents said yes?"

He nodded and looked apologetic. "I was

surprised. They think it's a great opportunity because they never have money for things like that. Gui's going, too. Why can't you come?"

Disappointment smothered Max all over again. "You know Papá. He worries about everything. He said that he and Buelo could train me as well as anyone else."

"That's true. But it won't be the same without you. Can't you convince him to change his mind? Maybe if you tell him my parents said yes?"

Max shook his head and tried not to cry. Once Papá's mind was set, there was no changing it. He stared up at the white clouds and watched his summer, his friends, and his plans drift away.

"It's okay, hermano. I promise I'll remember all the fancy drills so we can practice together on weekends." Chuy tried to console him. "And we can still go to the water hole."

Max nodded and avoided Chuy's eyes. He choked out his words. "Do you want to practice?"

"I can't. I only came to tell you Ortiz invited us

all to stay at his cousin's tonight and have dinner with the new coach. I have to watch my sisters before I catch the bus. But . . . meet at the fork on Saturday? Three o'clock?"

"Sure." Max put his hand in his pocket and felt the leche quemada. Even through the wax paper, he could tell the candy had already flattened and started to crumble. He didn't bother to offer it to Chuy.

When Chuy turned to leave, he almost toppled Papá.

"Nice to see you, Chuy. Ready to chase some balls?"

"Sorry, Señor Córdoba. I can't today." He ran off.

"Where's he going?"

Tears stung Max's eyes. "You were wrong! His parents said yes to the clinic. They said it was a great opportunity! Gui's parents said yes, too. And Chuy and Gui get to have dinner with the new coach tonight. You never let me do *anything*! Or go anywhere on my own!"

"Max, when you're older—"

"What does *that* mean? When will I *ever* be old enough?"

"In time. I promise . . . And don't worry about Chuy." Papá held up two fingers and pressed them together. "You two will always be like brothers."

Max frowned. "Until he and Gui and Ortiz make the team and I don't."

"You'll practice. You'll do your best. Then, what will be—"

"I *know*, Papá, what will be will be!" Max hung his head. He dropped the ball and dribbled it out onto the field. He didn't want Papá to see him crying or to lecture him to act like a man, especially when he treated him like a baby. He dribbled the ball from one end of the field to the other and back again. Finally, he passed it to Papá.

"Let's do some drills. You said Ortiz was better at kicking and throwing. So we will practice throwing. Did you know it can be more accurate than kicking?"

Max shook his head, grateful Papá didn't mention his red eyes.

"It's true. Get into the box so I can toss some balls at you. You save the shot, and then immediately bring back your throwing arm. With your non-throwing arm, point down the field to where you want the ball to go. Then, using all your strength, heave it. The top goalies can throw half the length of the field. Afterward, we can practice shooting on goal, just in case you want to play forward."

Max went through the motions, but his heart wasn't in it. He imagined Chuy, Gui, and Ortiz on the bus every day together, and all the fun they'd have at the clinic making friends with boys from other towns. And how they'd meet Coach Cruz before the tryouts. All without him.

"Max!" called Papá.

He was so lost in his misery, he didn't realize Papá had stopped throwing balls. He waved Max forward and put a protective arm around him. "Today isn't a good day for concentrating. But I have been thinking about what you asked me yesterday."

Max looked up.

"I *could* use your help at the ruins tomorrow."

"But you said it was no place for a boy."

"You reminded me that you are almost twelve, and maybe that is old enough."

"Really?" Max knew Papá was just trying to take the sting away from not going to the clinic. But still, Max would be the first boy ever to cross the gates. It wasn't much, but it was something. "Thank you."

Papá tousled Max's hair. "You might not thank me after you realize what hard work it is."

Seven

The chessboard lay open on the old picnic table beneath the oak tree in the side yard—the soapstone rooks, knights, bishops, pawns, king, and queen in a huddle, waiting to be positioned.

"Maximiliano!"

"Hola, Tío."

"How is my favorite nephew?" he asked, squeezing Max in a hug. His bushy white eyebrows, mustache, and soft round body made him look like a gentle San Nicolás.

"You don't have any other nephews."

"Then it *is* true. You are my favorite!" His booming laugh filled the yard. Within arm's reach, a plate was piled high with empanadas.

His aunties sat in chairs at either end of the table. They were both as tall as Max and as thin.

Amelia spread her arms wide, folding Max beneath her protective wings. "Hola, mi cariño, my love." She was Buelo's older sister and had once been a nurse. Her enormous eyes beneath dark-rimmed glasses made her look like a curious wren.

She held up a crossword puzzle book. "You will help me later?"

Max nodded and then ran to Mariana, Buelo's younger sister, who was teaching him to garden and cook.

"I made rellenos for dinner, from the chiles we planted!" she said, hugging him, too. "After they bake, you can dress them with the sauce and sprinkle the cheese. Remember how I taught you?"

"Yes," said Max, grinning. "And I remember how to eat them, too."

She patted his face, cooing. "You appreciate food because you help grow and prepare it. Now tell me, is it true you will be your father's apprentice?"

He smiled half-heartedly and nodded. "Papá is taking me to the ruins tomorrow."

She raised her eyebrows. "The day has come."

Papá slid in across from Tío and pointed to the

empanadas. "You know, Rodrigo, I'm beginning to think our Sunday dinners are just an excuse to convince Amelia to stop at the bakery. Tell the truth."

"I'll never admit such a thing, Junior!" He picked up an empanada and licked a dollop of filling oozing from the small turnovers. He nodded toward the plate. "Maximiliano, they're pineapple, your favorite."

Max grabbed one and looked at Papá. "Please?"

"Just one," said Papá. "Don't spoil your dinner." He began setting up the chess pieces on the board.

Buelo came from the cottage with glasses and a pitcher of lemonade.

"Considering the speed of gossip in Santa Maria," said Tío, "I suppose you've all heard about the new coach, Héctor Cruz?"

"Oh, yes," said Mariana. "Everyone is talking."

Amelia nodded. "I wonder how he will adjust here."

"Why?" asked Max.

"He's coming from a big city," said Tío. "We're a sleepy little village, a walking town where most distances are more quickly covered on foot, or in a wagon with a sure-footed burro."

"Some people have trucks or cars," said Max.

Mariana held up a finger. "And there are buses to San Clemente, where a train can take you anywhere."

"We are not entirely cut off," said Buelo, setting a glass in front of each of them and sitting down. "Almost everyone in the village has a phone. It is just here in the foothills we do not have service."

"Yes, of course all that is true," said Tío. "But he's a young coach and probably ambitious. He may want something bigger and better. It would be good for the village if he stayed for at least a few seasons though, especially for our boys who want to make the team this year and move up in the league."

"*I* want to make the team this year and move up," said Max, glancing at Papá.

Tío cleared his throat. "There was a council meeting yesterday. We've had a letter from Coach Cruz. Seems he's a stickler for details. We must be sure to enforce the league rules about who is eligible to play. Which means we need to have all the documents on file. No exceptions."

"Like birth certificates," said Max. "That's what Ortiz said."

"Yes." Tío's eyes darted to Papá.

Papá picked up the white queen and tapped it on the table, the rhythm like a ticking clock.

Buelo reached over and covered his hand.

A thick silence settled. Max could hear himself chewing.

"Given the recent circumstances, Junior," said Tío, "and since you two are going to the ruins tomorrow, it would be wise to—"

Papá shook his head. "Not yet."

Mariana leaned toward Papá. "Junior, he needs to be prepared."

Amelia set her glasses on the table and rubbed her eyes. "I agree."

Max looked at their concerned faces. "What are you talking about?"

Papá turned to him. "I need to talk to Tío and

your aunties. Get started on Lola's bath. When you're done, it will be almost time for dinner."

"If it's about me, why can't I hear?"

Papá gave him a look that said the conversation was over.

Max raised his hands, palms up, as if to ask why, then dropped them. He knew it was useless to argue. Reluctantly, he whistled for Lola and headed toward the shed next to Dulce's corral.

As soon as Lola saw him dragging out the big metal tub, she pranced and ran in circles. After he filled it with the hose, Max gave the command and she jumped in.

Max could see Papá, Tío, Buelo, and his aunties huddled together at the table, talking. The veil of secrecy again. What did they know? And what had Mariana meant when she said he needed to be prepared?

Prepared for what?

Eight

Overnight, fog wrapped Santa Maria in a soft blanket.

The trees were murky shadows, the world—silent. Not even the birds chirped. Were the rumors true? Had the ghosts of the hidden ones arrived on the wings of the peregrine? Within the mist, would Max hear their prayers and feel their presence?

He found Papá and Buelo hitching Dulce to the wagon.

"Good morning, my son." Papá's eyes were dark and weary-looking beneath his straw hat. He put a water jug and brown bag through the slats of the wagon into the flat bed and led Dulce toward the path.

Buelo plopped a hat like Papá's on Max's head, pointing to the eastern sky where a bright smear promised the sun would eventually burn through. "You need to get going before the day warms." Buelo hugged him goodbye.

At the fork, they started up the mountain on the dirt path that weaved through agave crowns and firethorn bushes. "When we get there, stay in the clearing and watch your step. I don't want to pull you from a crumbling pile of rocks like I once did for Buelo."

"I know. I'll be careful."

Papá lectured about precarious ledges and the importance of wearing work gloves to protect from spiders, rusty nails, and cracked stones. "I want to make something clear, Max. You are never, *ever* to come to the ruins alone. Do you understand?"

Before he could stop himself, Max blurted, "Because of the ghosts of the hidden ones."

"Because it's dangerous. If there are ghosts, they are the ones we bring with us."

"How can we *bring* a ghost with us?"

"If a spirit lives on, Max, it is in someone's mind, not in a place."

There was something comforting about Papá's confidence. But how could he be so sure about the ghosts when everyone else in the village was convinced otherwise?

It was slow going with Dulce and the wagon. After almost an hour of climbing the switchbacks, they came upon a wrought-iron gate with spear-shaped finials and fencing that stretched in either direction like a parade of stalwart soldiers. Papá pushed open the gate and brought the wagon through. The road widened, separating two groves of coral trees, their intricate branches dotted with flaming blooms. Parrots swooped and squawked. At the edge of the trees, Papá stopped and pointed to a vast clearing. "There it is, Max. The ruins and La Reina Gigante."

The sun had overcome the fog, and the cliff top was bright and dewy. At the far edge of the rubble, on the cliff overlooking the village, La Reina Gigante stood majestic. Her height was staggering, every stone intact, the masonry interrupted only by a large wooden door and the loopholes where guards once stood watch, or shot at attackers. Red bougainvillea crawled up her face.

A gentle breeze sent a few red petals sailing above him, just like in his dream. He gazed up. The tower was even more imposing up close, yet at the same time familiar and welcoming.

"How is she still standing when everything else has crumbled?"

"It *is* amazing that all five stories are intact, isn't it? Engineers think the tower was built by different artisans than the ones who built the palace. The construction is far superior. It's been checked and the foundation is sound."

Max pointed to the very top, where sticks, dried grass, and feathers spilled through the crenels.

"Peregrine's scrape. It looks like our friend is nesting," Papá said, then handed Max a pair of work gloves. "Let's get busy."

Max followed Papá through the clearing. Weeds and thistle grew through yesterday's cobblestones. Pyramids of rock rose up where walls had collapsed. Blackberry vines choked the side of a well. Yet a whisper of the palace's beauty was still there in the magnificent shell and the remaining walls that once surrounded grand rooms. Even the cobwebs looked like veiled curtains.

Papá carefully considered different mounds of stone. "These," he said of the round gray ones. "And those." He pointed to the white rocks that might have once been chiseled for a fireplace. Papá picked up a few of each, starting piles. "I'll drag them from the debris. You cart them."

For over an hour, as Papá sorted, Max carried the heavy stones to the bed of the wagon. With each trip, he gazed at the tower, which stood defiant in the midst of all that had fallen around it. *Was* it protected by spirits?

He was grateful when Papá called for a break. His arms already ached. They sat in the shade of the tower on a low wall, where Papá had left the jug of water and the bag. They took off their hats and work gloves and ate the burritos Buelo had packed.

When they were almost done, Papa said, "Max, have you heard that people hid here during the war?"

Max nodded and looked out over the ruins. He tried to imagine being stranded in a place like this. "How did they survive?"

"The tower was a safe apartment. And the well worked. On the other side of the ruins, there are remains from an old chicken coop and a small goat pen, so there were eggs and milk. And as you can see, berries. But there were people ... helpers who brought them provisions, too."

Max finished chewing his last bite, then stood on the stone wall and walked back and forth, balancing with his arms out. "You mean the Guardians of the Hidden Ones?"

Papá nodded and cleared his throat. "Yes."

Max jumped off the wall and stood in front of Papá. "The guardians were fearless. They were secret warriors for justice. They were brave and determined and—"

"Slow down, Max. The guardians aren't ... weren't warriors for justice so much as an underground network who helped the hidden ones cross safely through Santa Maria, mainly during the war in Abismo. Back then, there was a dictator who punished anyone who opposed him. Many people fled and crossed into Santa Maria. But our government didn't like all the people coming through, so they passed the Harboring Law, making it illegal for them to stay, and for anyone to help or hide them."

"Were any guardians or hidden ones ever caught?"

"Not in Santa Maria, but elsewhere, yes. The guardians were sent to jail and the hidden ones were sent back to Abismo, to whatever terrible fate awaited them."

"That's awful," said Max. "Ortiz said the hidden ones were murderers and thieves, and the guardians were criminals, too, because they broke the law by protecting them. Is that true?"

Papá bristled. "The guardians helped for compassionate reasons. And the hidden ones were *not* murderers or thieves. They were soldiers who fought on the wrong side of a dictator, and innocent women and children."

"How do you know?"

Papá searched his eyes. "Because Buelo, Tío, Amelia, and Mariana . . . were the original Guardians of the Hidden Ones."

Max's mouth dropped open. Buelo walked with a cane. His aunties often needed help opening a jar. And Tío huffed when he walked uphill. How could they be guardians?

"I know it's hard to imagine, but they were much younger then. Don't be deceived by how time has changed them. They are still strong and capable."

Max grinned, feeling a surge of pride. "Papá, they're heroes! I can't wait to tell Chuy! Everyone should know what they—"

"Max! *No one* must *ever* find out. You may talk *only* to Buelo about this, and in private. Do you understand?" The look on Papá's face was sobering.

"So, no one *ever* knew?" asked Max.

"Over the years, there have been people in the village who've made pointed comments to Buelo, Tío, and your aunties. I think there were those who suspected them, but nothing has ever come of the gossip. That's why you mustn't ever say anything. Even now, it would be dangerous to expose us."

"Us? Were you?"

"On occasion, yes. And your mother—"

"My *mother* was a guardian?" Max's mind leaped. She was a hero, too! He imagined a valiant caped protector helping those in need.

"She escorted two young women to the next safe place. And never came home."

Max's stomach turned. "Was she caught? Is she in jail . . . or dead?"

"No, no. Nothing like that. When I searched for her, I was told she had continued on with them."

Papá looked distraught. He leaned forward, propping his elbows on his knees and holding his head in his hands.

Max sank to the wall next to him. "Papá, what is it?"

Papá's eyes begged forgiveness. He took a deep breath. "Before your mother and I moved back to

Santa Maria, we lived in San Clemente. That's where you were born. A doctor came to the house to deliver you. Afterward, he signed a notice of live birth, which we were supposed to take to the municipal offices to file for a birth certificate. But when your mother left, she took everything."

The truth slowly wormed its way into Max's mind.

"I . . . I don't have a birth certificate?"

Papá shook his head.

"But how can I play fútbol? Tío said everyone must prove their age. No exceptions."

Papá winced. "I know."

The repercussions mushroomed. "How could I ever move up to a club team? Or any team ever again? I will need a birth certificate for other things, too, won't I? To work or drive or—"

"Max, stop. Please. Tomorrow I'm going to San Clemente to take care of the matter once and for all. I should have resolved this long ago."

"How long will you be gone?"

"Things move slowly in the municipal offices. I'll have to fill out forms, make appointments, and meet with the authorities. Hopefully no more than two weeks."

Max jumped up and stood in front of Papá. "*Hopefully*? The tryouts are in four weeks and four days! How could you let this happen?"

Papá ran his hands through his hair. His face paled. What was he not saying?

"Tell me." Max pressed. "I'm old enough to know!"

Papá closed his eyes and gathered himself. "First things first . . ."

"Then stone by stone. I *know*, Papá!"

"I'll explain everything when I return. And don't worry, Max. It will be *fine*. It will." Papá sounded as if he was trying to convince himself. He reached out and grabbed Max's hand and held it tight. "You have every right to be angry. But now we need to focus on the task at hand. We have a bridge to build. And we need the job. I'm counting on you to work for me. And to stay under Buelo's watch, and not go anywhere without telling him. Otherwise I cannot go to San Clemente with peace of mind and take care of this. I've already talked to Buelo. You two will have to accomplish a lot while I'm gone. And you'll have to be patient. Can you do that?"

Max yanked his hand from Papá's.

"Max, answer me. Can you do what I ask?"

What choice did he have?

Nine

Max turned away from Papá and faced the tower. "I want to go inside. Am I old enough to do that?"

Papá hesitated, then walked to the wooden door and heaved it open. "For just a few minutes."

Max stepped across the tower's threshold.

The air was cool and the light dim, except for slits of sunlight from the loopholes. Dirt, dried leaves, and chicken feathers littered the cobbled floor. Max understood why someone would hide here. The tower was a fortress, safe and impenetrable. "Hello!" he called, his voice sounding hollow in the cavernous womb.

He walked around the room, running his fingers over the mortared walls, tracing one of the stones. They were larger than the ones used on bridges. These were oblong with a beveled edge. The construction *was* superior. At the arched stairwell opening, a padlocked iron gate blocked the way. Max peered through the rails at the narrow corridor spiraling upward. There were markings on some of the stones, but they were too far away to read.

He leaned against the gate and closed his eyes, his thoughts twisting like the staircase. He pulled the compass from beneath his shirt and held it tight. What if Papá *couldn't* take care of the matter in San Clemente? What if it *wasn't* fine?

A wind threaded through the loopholes, and a shushing noise began to pulse through the tower. It reminded Max of the time Tío had taken him to the ocean and held a conch shell to his ear. The sound grew louder and more insistent.

Arrorró. Arrorró. Arrorró.

Hush. Hush. Hush. There was a lullaby that began that way. He tried to remember the words.

Arrorró, mi niño. "Hush, my son," he whispered. That's how the song began. Was La Reina singing? Or a ghost? A wail, like a baby's cry, sent a cold shiver down his back. Heart pounding, Max fled the room and ran into the clearing, the compass thumping against his chest.

Papá stopped sorting stones. "You okay?"

"I heard strange noises . . ."

"It's just the wind working its way through the chinks. Makes La Reina Gigante moan and sing. Up here, even an animal's cry can carry. And every time a cloud shifts, it looks as though someone is standing in the shadows." Papá shook his head. "It's no wonder all the rumors of ghosts."

Max nodded. It had felt like more than that. He took a deep breath. "Why is the gate inside locked?"

"Tío wants to preserve the tower. Someday make it a monument. A lot of history happened here."

"What are the markings on the wall?"

"People scratched their names and messages on the stones so loved ones who followed would know they had made it this far. Or just to show they were once here."

"Can you take me up there?"

"No." Papá rubbed his forehead. "We're never to disturb anything in the tower. Besides, it's not safe." He closed the wooden door and walked to the wagon, where he flung a tarp over the bed of stones and tied it down.

"But you said the tower was sound."

"There's really nothing up there that concerns you. Come. Dulce can't pull more. Let's head out. I have a lot to do before I leave in the morning, and I need to talk to Buelo about the bridge work." Papá led Dulce from the clearing.

Frustration squeezed Max as he followed Papá and the wagon. A twig snapped behind him and the bushes rustled. When he turned, he thought he saw a shadowy figure dart to the outskirts of the ruins.

The falcon swooped overhead, its wide wings shadowing the vision. When the bird veered, whatever Max thought he saw had disappeared. Was it only a cloud shadow as Papá had said? Or something else?

The heat of the day and everything Papá had shared pressed in on him. His mind was a bulging suitcase overstuffed with questions and secrets.

Ten

As soon as Papá left on the Tuesday morning bus for San Clemente, Amelia and Mariana arrived with purpose, armed with baskets stuffed with vegetables, recipes, and crossword puzzle books.

Miss Domínguez came and went, too, with homemade bread, and as always, a book to read out loud at the table. After lunch, Mariana and Amelia headed home and Tío arrived, staying past bedtime. All week, it was the same. There was always someone sharing a meal, riding along in the wagon while they hauled stones to the new site, or watching from the sidelines as Max completed the fútbol drills that Buelo dictated from his chair in the shade.

By Saturday, the heat wallowed and fell upon them in waves—the sun's breath was hot and thick. The water hole beckoned, and Chuy was waiting at the fork at three o'clock as planned. When he saw Max, he grinned and took off running down the road.

Setting aside his burdens, Max chased after him. "Wait for me!"

They picked up speed, then at a bend, stopped and looked into a ravine below. Last summer, Chuy's mom had sent them to pick wild raspberries. Down the steep embankment, they'd discovered a hidden pond in a shady grotto with a natural mud slide cascading into it.

"There!" said Chuy. Halfway down the bank, the wild berry bushes sprawled along the hillside.

They found the top of the gully and stripped down to their shorts.

Max let out a whoop and pushed off. The cold mud slid him forward, faster and faster. He leaned into the last turn and waved his arms. With a huge splash, he landed in the water. He swam to the side and Chuy followed.

They ran up and slid down the hill a dozen times, shoving and splashing each other before finally climbing onto a large flat rock. They stretched out on their stomachs, like basking lizards.

Chuy dragged his fingers in the pool. "The water feels great after practicing all week in the heat." He caught himself. "Sorry. I didn't mean to mention the clinic. I wish you were there, too."

"It's okay," said Max. "How is it anyway?"

Chuy turned on his side and propped up on one elbow. "The days are long. We catch the bus early in the morning and we don't get home until almost dinner. And you should see Ortiz, strutting around the field and reminding everyone that he's the manager's cousin."

Max flipped on his back and smiled. "I can just see the fanfarrón."

"I've been practicing to play center back. That way if you get goalie, I can play right in front of you and clean up balls the other defenders let through. Make you look good."

"And I'll save all the balls *you* let through and make the entire team look good!"

Water trickled. Dragonflies fluttered. Birds whistled. For a moment, Max could almost imagine it was last summer and he didn't have a care in the world.

"I got a pair of Volantes," said Chuy. "The coach had some from players who only wore them in tournaments. They're like new."

Max buried his envy. "That's great. Hopefully I'll have a pair soon, too."

"Every afternoon at the clinic there's a scrimmage. The coaches divided us into two teams. Gui and Ortiz and I are together."

Max was growing weary of the clinic talk. "Guess what? I went to the ruins. And I went inside the tower."

Chuy sat up, wide-eyed. "You did?"

Max told him about the site and the noises in the tower.

"So there *are* ghosts," said Chuy.

"I definitely heard things and felt a presence, but you know Papá. He wouldn't admit to anything."

"But you *heard* them. What did they sound like?"

Max lowered his voice. "Whispering and sad crying. It was creepy. And I thought I saw someone, or *something*, standing near the tower. Then it just . . . disappeared."

Chuy gasped. "I knew it. Everyone says so. Do you think it was the ghost of a hidden one?"

A shiver ran through Max. "Maybe . . ."

Just then, they heard a shriek and both boys startled.

"What was that?" Chuy rubbed his arms. "I got goose bumps."

Max's head whipped around. In a blur, someone flew down the mud slide and splashed into the pool. Then another splash. A boy sprang up, spewing water like a fountain. It was Ortiz, and Gui was right behind him.

Max looked at Chuy in disbelief. "You *told* them about the water hole?"

Chuy shook his head. "I didn't. I swear." He stood up. "What are you guys doing here?"

"Ortiz and I went to your house," said Gui. "Your mom said you and Max went swimming near the raspberries."

"We followed the yelling and splashing," said Ortiz. "It wasn't that hard to find. Wow. This is a *great* spot." He swam across to them, slicing the water and sending it splattering over their heads. "How come you guys never mentioned it?"

Max and Chuy didn't answer.

Ortiz climbed out of the pool and joined them on the rock. "I heard your father went to San Clemente to prove you're a person."

Max froze. How did Ortiz know?

"My dad's on the council. Mayor Soto told him your dad went to get a copy of your birth certificate. Guess everyone is scrambling with the new rules. Better hope he returns before tryouts."

"Don't worry. He'll be back in plenty of time," said Max, relieved that Ortiz didn't ask questions about why he didn't have one at home.

"Less competition for me if he isn't." Ortiz flopped back into the water.

"Pay no attention to him," said Chuy. "The coach told us there was a boy who didn't have a birth certificate because it was lost in a fire. The league accepted his baptism papers from the church, and a letter signed by people who knew him from birth. And there was another boy who used his hospital record. But it had to be notarized."

Since Max was born at home, there wouldn't be any hospital records. But there was a photo somewhere of Papá holding him on the steps of Our Lady of Sorrows on the day he was baptized, so there must be a record. Had Papá thought of that?

Ortiz climbed from the pool and started uphill. "Chuy and Gui, let's go for some leche quemada. I'll buy. Remember what our coach said about teammates. The more time we spend together on and off the field, the better we'll play as a team."

Chuy stood up.

"Are you leaving?" asked Max. "We just got here."

Chuy shrugged. "Our coach did say that. Do you want to come?"

When Max didn't answer, Chuy scrambled uphill, waved, and called, "See you next Saturday!"

Ortiz waved, too, and affectionately rubbed Chuy's head. Then he hugged Chuy to his side and mimicked his voice. "See you next Saturday!"

Max lowered himself from the rock into the water, swimming beneath the surface. When he came up for air, Chuy, Ortiz, and Gui were gone. As he climbed from the pool and dressed, he thought about what Papá had said, that he and Chuy would always be like brothers. It didn't feel like it anymore.

A strange knot of hurt shadowed Max. On the way home, he pounded the path to the cottage, trying to outrun the feeling.

But it followed, nipping at him like a hungry goat.

Eleven

"Buelo, where's my baptism record?" asked Max as he burst into the cottage.

Buelo looked up from where he sat on the sofa, lacing his work boots. Max could tell by his flushed cheeks and mussed hair that he'd just woken from a nap. "I am not sure. Why?"

Max put his hands on his hips. "I *have* a baptism record, right?"

"Of course. Your father has it somewhere. What is this about?"

"Sometimes you can use your baptism record from the church to register for fútbol if you don't have a birth certificate."

"Where did you hear that?"

"Chuy's coach told him. Can I look for mine, in case Papá doesn't get back in time?"

Buelo frowned. "I do not believe it would serve any purpose. Anyway, it is probably with the personal papers your father keeps. He would not want anyone going through them unless it was an emergency." He stood and grabbed his sun hat. "If he is not home in time for the tryouts, I will look on your behalf. Now, come." Buelo clapped his hands. "I am feeling energetic. The heat has let up, and I want to start preparing the wood for the falsework. Let us see how much we can get done before dinner, shall we?"

Max followed Buelo into the yard. He didn't understand why they couldn't look for the baptism record now. If they found it, Max could stop worrying.

Buelo gave instructions and Max set up the saw-horses and laid the wood planks across them. He measured and marked a line in chalk, then carried each length to the battered workbench where Buelo used the handsaw to cut it. Max carefully loaded the wood into the wagon, stacking it by size so it could be unloaded the same way, exactly as Papá would have done.

"Once we finish cutting this wood, we will haul it to the site and build the arched wooden hull," said Buelo. "When your father gets back, we will begin the stonework over the falsework, building symmetrically from the abutments toward the center."

"I know," said Max. "And after the stones are mortared, and the bridge is built, we will remove the falsework to reveal the tunnel."

Buelo laughed. "I suppose you have watched us enough times." A shadow passed over him and he glanced up. "It looks like your friend is paying us a visit."

The peregrine hovered above them.

Buelo craned his neck. "Isn't she a magnificent pilgrim?"

Max nodded. "I saw her nest at the top of La Reina when I was at the ruins."

All the questions and secrets crammed in his mind flooded back to him. Papá had said he could talk only to Buelo about such things, and in private. He looked around the yard. "Where's Tío?"

"He has a council meeting this afternoon, so we are on our own."

"Buelo, Papá said I could ask you when we were alone about Los Guardianes de los Escondidos. Was it exciting to be a guardian?"

Buelo stopped sawing. "I was wondering how long it would take you to ask. The truth? It was far more dangerous than exciting. And a huge responsibility."

"Were there a lot of hidden ones?"

"When I was a young man during and after the war, there was a big wave, mostly soldiers and their families. And then for twenty years, while your father was growing up, only a handful. But there was another wave after that. We called it the Brigade of Women."

"It was all women?"

"Yes. Some babies and small children, too."

"Why did *they* run away? Was there another war?"

"A different type of oppression. Countrymen

fighting countrymen about what a woman could and could not do. Some of the women were mothers whose families had banished them because there was no father to support them. Others wished to escape their husbands who had mistreated them. Some were servants who were considered less than human. We hid them in the tower and, as quickly as we could, secretly moved them to the next safe place."

"But the war was over by then. Why couldn't you tell anyone?"

"The law. It was, and still is, illegal to harbor people fleeing other countries. In some places it is even illegal to be compassionate and provide water or directions to a fugitive. But they were in grave danger. Some of the men from Abismo—who considered the women their property—came after them or hired people to find them. They would show a picture around and offer rewards. People talk for money. How could we not protect them?"

"Why would anyone come *here* to look?"

"There are only a few villages and towns between Abismo and the bigger cities north, east, and west of here," said Buelo. "Santa Maria is small, but it is on the way to everywhere."

"Did any of the hidden ones ever stay?"

"We are too close to Abismo for comfort. And there is greater safety and opportunity in the bigger cities where they could hide in plain sight, working and living like everyone else. If they had tried to stay in a small village like Santa Maria, and people discovered they were from Abismo, they would have been shunned. Spit upon. Or worse. It only takes one or two people to generate hate and make it escalate. I do not like to admit it, but there are people here in Santa Maria who have been my neighbors for years who behave that way."

"Ortiz said bad things about the hidden ones. What were they really like?"

"No two had the same story. But generally speaking, they had all been on a difficult journey for weeks on foot. Sometimes separated from their families. Tired, frightened, anxious. Angry at injustice. Sad to be leaving their homeland but wanting a new life, a different tomorrow."

"That must have been hard for them."

Buelo nodded. "No matter their disposition, though, I had to be calm and reassuring. And stay focused on delivering them safely. Anything could happen along the way, and I had to be ready to improvise at any moment."

"Did you take them in a car or a truck?"

"No. Too dangerous. There are always checkpoints for vehicles. On foot, we were safer and could get to places that were better hidden. Places a police car could never access."

Max shuddered. "If it was so dangerous, why did you do it?"

"I felt a moral obligation. How could I ignore their predicament?"

Max turned the information over in his mind. Could he risk his own life, knowing that he might end up in jail, just to make someone else's life better?

"Did any of them ever come back?"

"They could not chance it. And that always tugged at my heart. During the journey, there were those who kept their distance and put a wall between us the entire trip. But more often, by the time we arrived at our destination, we had become friends. It is sometimes easier to tell a stranger about yourself, especially one you are never going to see again, than it is to share your secrets with those closest to you. Knowing their stories and being their friend made saying goodbye difficult. I like to think, though, that their spirits return to La Reina Gigante, like they say . . . on the wings of the peregrine."

"So you believe it?"

"Of course I do. It comforts me."

"When I was at the tower, *I heard* the whispering."

"I believe you. You were brave to go inside."

"I didn't even go beyond the locked gate and I was scared. But I guess the tower would seem welcoming if I were running away from Abismo. *You* were the brave one, Buelo, to be a guardian."

"Well, it was worth finding the courage . . . to give people hope. To show them that the world is not all ugliness, but holds beauty and goodness. Being a guardian is not about borders or laws or money. We never took money. It's about people helping people."

Max turned all the details over in his mind. "How did they get into the tower?"

"The key is hidden behind some thorny vines where no one would accidentally find it. I'll show you someday."

"And then where did you take them?"

"Far away. It took three overnights to reach the next safe place."

"Did you ever keep going, to see where the hidden ones ended up?"

Buelo shook his head. "There is a strict code among the guardians. We take the hidden ones *only* to the next safe place. We cannot assist farther unless that guardian asks for help. This protects the privacy of the hidden ones. Believe me, they do not want to be found." Buelo stretched. "That is enough for today. Help me put away the tools."

Max followed closely behind, gathering his courage. "Papá said my mother was a guardian."

"Well . . . yes."

"Why was she allowed to break the code and travel on?"

Buelo rubbed his eyes. "That is not for me to say."

Max persisted. "The other day, Papá didn't tell me everything. Do you know what else there is?"

"Maximiliano, your father will discuss such things with you when the time is right."

"Buelo, what's the difference if I know now or when he returns? Please tell me," begged Max. "Or I can ask Tío and my aunties . . ."

Buelo turned and held up a hand to signal Max to stop. His eyes filled with a look Max had never seen before. Was it anger? Or fear? "You will do *nothing* of the kind. You will wait for your father. Besides, they would never interfere." He took his handkerchief from his pocket and blotted his forehead. "I said that was enough for today. The heat is catching up to me. I need to go inside."

In his entire life, Max had never heard Buelo speak with such fierceness. There was no reason to press. Buelo wasn't going to budge.

Max cleaned the yard and played with Lola.

At dinner, Buelo was quieter than usual and for the first time that Max could remember, he said he was too tired for storytelling and went to bed early.

Later, when Max could hear Buelo snoring, he stood at the window in his room, looked up at La Reina Gigante, and said his usual prayers. Then he placed the compass on the sill with the face up. The needle bobbed north, pointing straight at the giant queen and beyond. Was his mother in the north? Was that what Papá and Buelo were hiding—the name of the place she now lived?

Or were they keeping something more from him?

Twelve

Another week threatened to pass, much like the one before, with no news from San Clemente.

"What is taking Papá so long?" demanded Max. He led Dulce and the wagon filled with wood down the hill toward the new bridge site. Buelo sat on the wagon's tailgate, hitching a ride to the Saturday market. Lola trotted behind.

"Patience," said Buelo. "We knew it would take some time. The tryouts are still almost three weeks away."

Max kicked at the dirt. His summer was nothing he'd hoped for.

Just before the village, Buelo climbed down and patted his shoulder. "Are you sure you can unload the wood by yourself and get Dulce home?"

"Buelo, I already *said* I'd lift one board at a time," said Max. "And even Lola could lead stubborn old Dulce."

Buelo patted Dulce's neck. "Max doesn't mean it, sweet girl. He's just bad tempered of late. I know you're as reliable as the sun."

Max rolled his eyes.

"After the market, I'll have lunch with Mariana. Don't worry about picking me up. I'll get a ride or walk home."

Max nudged the burro forward without even waving goodbye.

At the bridge site, Max cleared a level place for the wood and put down a tarp. Lola promptly claimed a corner.

"Don't get too comfortable," said Max as he carried the lengths from the wagon to the tarp. When he needed more room, he ordered, "Off, Lola!"

She skulked away.

What was wrong with him? How could he yell at such an innocent animal? "Sorry, Lola . . . Come."

As he petted her muzzle, something sailed overhead and splashed in the river in front of them.

Max spun around.

"Relax, Max. It's just us." Ortiz and Gui ran past him to the river's edge, lobbing rocks into the water.

Chuy was right behind them. He stopped to pet Lola. "We saw Buelo in the village. He said you were here. We're going to the water hole. Want to come?"

"I can't," said Max. "I have work to do."

Chuy shifted uncomfortably from one foot to the other.

"What's wrong?" asked Max.

"Ortiz said if I didn't tell you, he would."

"Tell me what?"

Chuy lowered his voice. "Last night, Gui and I went to Ortiz's for dinner. All his mother talked about was the tryouts, and how Ortiz is the best goalie, and how the league is finally enforcing who can play and who can't. Then she started talking about your family. She said they're all criminals and should be reported. And that if the league finds out about their past, someone will have something to say about you playing on the team."

The blood drained from Max's face. Did Ortiz's mother know that Papá and Buelo had been guardians? And his aunts and uncle, too? Was she one of the people who had made pointed comments?

"What did *you* say?" asked Max.

Chuy looked helpless. "Nothing. I . . . I didn't know what they were talking about."

Ortiz and Gui walked toward them, shoving each other and laughing.

Max stepped forward. "Ortiz, your mother should mind her own business. She doesn't know *anything* about my family!"

"Didn't mean to upset you or throw you off your game," said Ortiz. "Just doing you a favor. *I'd* want to know if my family was full of criminals."

Fury rose up in Max. "They're *heroes*. But your mother? She's a gossip and a liar!"

Ortiz lunged at Max and shoved him to the ground.

Max jumped up, swinging.

Ortiz blocked Max's punches and knocked Max down again.

Lola bared her teeth and growled at Ortiz.

"Sit, Lola!" called Max. This was his fight.

Max stood and set his fists, expecting Ortiz to come after him.

Instead, he walked away. "Come on, Gui. Chuy."

Max watched him go, Ortiz's words thrumming in his ears.

He felt Chuy tug on his arm and he spun around, yelling, "You've known our family your *entire* life! How could you not defend us, no matter what? I thought you were my friend!"

Chuy looked as if someone had slapped him. "I *am*."

Max shook his head in disbelief. "No. You're like a little stray dog following at Ortiz's heels because he invited you to the fútbol clinic, and you got new shoes, and he buys you leche quemada, and brings you to dinner at the big house."

Chuy's face fell.

Max turned back to the wagon and started unloading the wood. As he grabbed the last plank, he paused, feeling unsteady. Could Papá or Buelo go to jail for being guardians so many years ago?

A dark qualm slithered from a hole in his mind. It leered and taunted him. Then the ugly doubt slipped back into its hiding place. Max's hands trembled. The wood slid and thudded to the ground, leaving a long, thick splinter in the pad of his thumb. He gasped at the sharp pain.

Chuy rushed to his side.

"Leave me alone!"

After Chuy walked away, Max gritted his teeth and pulled out the long sliver of wood. Blood puddled in his palm.

He wrapped his hand in a rag and tugged Dulce to the cottage as fast as she could go with the wagon. Words can never hurt you. That's what everyone always said. Sticks and stones, yes. But not words.

They were wrong.

Thirteen

Max poured rubbing alcohol on the wound, cringing from the sting. Anger and determination stifled the hurt.

Papá kept anything of importance in a large metal box on the top shelf of his bedroom closet. His baptism record had to be there. He knew he shouldn't be rummaging, but he needed to settle this once and for all. Max stood on a chair, lifted down the box, and set it on the bed.

On top was an oilskin pouch. Papá's work map of the Santa Maria area was the only thing inside. When Papá and Buelo were given a commission for a new span, they spread it out on the kitchen table and pored over it to consider the best spot to build. Small numbered circles on the map indicated the existing Córdoba bridges with a corresponding numbered key in the margins. Max quickly glanced at the first few names and notes Papá had meticulously written.

1. Brookside Bridge—shallow and muddy channel
2. Arroyo Bridge—market road access
3. Maldonado's Bridge—dry bed during summer

He noticed little black stars had been inked on the map in various places along the river. Probably Buelo's favorite fishing spots. Max put the map back in the pouch and tossed it on the bed.

One by one, he sorted through his school report cards, invoices for bridge supplies, and receipts for tools. He found registrations for school events and sports teams.

Finally, he found the photo of Papá holding him on the steps of the church. It was hard to tell how old he was because of the long white christening gown he wore, but he wasn't an infant like most babies when they were baptized. Underneath the photo was a gold-trimmed certificate. At the top was the church's name, Our Lady of Sorrows. It certified that Maximiliano Feliciano Esteban Córdoba had been baptized by Father Marco Jiménez, and that his godparents were Amelia and Rodrigo Soto. But it was dated almost three years after Max was born. *After* his mother had left. The certificate didn't list Max's birth date or his parents' names. It recorded only the date of the baptism. Buelo had known it wouldn't help. If the league used this date as a birth record, he wouldn't even be old enough to try out.

Max dug deeper. Halfway through the box, he found a large unlabeled envelope. He pulled out a piece of brown paper. On it was a stone rubbing. It reminded him of the ones people made after a burial, when family members laid a piece of paper over the gravestone and rubbed with a thick-leaded pencil to copy the impression as a keepsake. But this was too small and mostly smudged and unreadable. Sometimes children carved their names in cobblestones on the street, but the outline of the rubbing was too large for that.

Max took the paper to the window and held it up to the light. His eyes widened as he was able to spell out a full word:

MAÑANALAND

He pressed the paper against the window pane. With effort, he deciphered a few more letters, but he could not string together another meaningful word. Carefully, he touched the marks. What was Mañanaland?

He backed away from the window and sat on the bed. Could the rubbing be from a bridge? Had Papá or Buelo named a bridge after someplace called Mañanaland?

He studied the paper. The etching was too close to the surface and not carefully wrought with a chisel, which a stonemason would have used on a spandrel or wing wall. And the shape of the stone wasn't typical of bridgework; it was oblong with a beveled edge. Where had he seen that?

The stones in La Reina Gigante had beveled edges. And the ones in the stairwell had markings that Papá had said were names and messages. If Max could get in there, he could compare this with those. Buelo said the key was hidden behind some thorny vines. He tried to picture the clearing, which was mostly rubble and weeds. He didn't remember many vines.

Max stood and paced. Papá had said there was nothing beyond the gate that concerned him. Yet this was important enough for Papá to keep it hidden away. So it must have *something* to do with his family. He folded the rubbing and slipped it into his pocket.

It was still early in the afternoon. He had time to get up the mountain and back before Buelo returned. Max knew he shouldn't go alone . . . but that was just Papá being overprotective.

He'd be careful.

Fourteen

Outside, Max whistled. "Come on, girl. Let's go for a walk!"

Lola sprang from her spot in the shade and ran to him, yelping with excitement.

She pranced along the path, stopping to relish the smells, and pouncing on every twig in her path. At the fork, they turned uphill toward the ruins, covering ground in half the time without Dulce and the wagon. Halfway up the switchbacks, Lola's head jerked toward the cliff. She planted her feet and barked.

Max moved closer to her, looping a finger through her collar. A cloud drifted overhead, shading them, then just as quickly moved aside for the sun. Max blew out a long breath. "Calm down, girl. It's just the shadows making you jumpy." But when they reached the property gates, Lola whined and refused to budge.

"I know, Lola. Papá wouldn't approve," said Max, unwrapping the chain. "But you're with me so I'm not alone. Besides, I've been here before."

He opened the gate just enough for the two of them to sidle through. "Come!" Max insisted.

When they reached the ruins, Max stood in the clearing with his hands on his hips, looking for thorny vines.

Bougainvillea climbed up the stones of the tower. When Max had helped Buelo trim the one at the cottage, he'd been snagged by its barbs many times. The base of the main stalk where the plant rooted seemed like a good hiding place. Max searched but found nothing. He poked around the wall to see if a key was hidden behind the sparse branches. Again nothing.

He hunted around the perimeter of the clearing. None of the trees or bushes had thorns. In the rubble, only grassy weeds poked through the stones. A bramble of blackberry vines crept along the well. Berries had prickly stems as sharp as thorns.

Max grabbed a stick and slowly walked around the well, lifting the branches until he spotted a brick not flush with the others. He carefully wriggled it from its space. There, nestled in the hollow, was the key!

He grabbed it and raced inside the tower to the gate in the stairwell. He slipped the key into the lock and turned. It clicked!

His heart pounded as he pushed open the gate and slowly climbed the stone steps, running his fingers along the etchings.

VALDEMARO SERVANO   *MAURICIO HERNANDEZ*

THE FIGHT REMAINS   *UNTIL THE NEXT BATTLE*

MERCEDES AND JESSE ARAYA

WE STAND TOGETHER

FATIMA PEÑA   *CÉSAR ROJAS*

BY GOD'S GRACE FREEDOM   *THE WAR IS NOT OVER*

On the second story, hundreds of names crawled up the wall like regiments of ants. So many soldiers. So many families. They must have been from the war. Some stones held just one name, large and bold—*DANTE*—as if screaming *I was here*. Others held a message. It would take hours to read them all. How many people had hidden here? Who were they and what were their stories? Had they ever reunited with their families?

GERTRUDA AND CARMEN LOSA
MAMA WE WILL WAIT FOR YOU

IN AN UNFORGIVING WORLD
I PRAY FOR LOVE, I PRAY FOR PEACE. LUPE PEREZ

BELTRAN V AND JUAN J
THANK YOU TO THOSE WHO SET US FREE

ESPERANZA O
LOST WITHOUT MY BELOVED

A breeze whistled as it threaded through the loopholes. Then, just as on his first visit, the shushing sound pulsed like a heartbeat.

Arrorró. Arrorró. Arrorró.

The muffled rhythm surrounded him. "It's just the wind working its way through the chinks," he reassured Lola. "Makes La Reina moan and sing."

Lola whined. Max patted her head. "It's okay, girl. It's a lullaby." More of the words flooded back to him. "Arrorró, mi niño. Arrorró, mi sol. Hush, my child. Hush, my sunshine . . ." He shivered as a high-pitched whistling began. Was a ghost singing to him again?

Lola began to bay, her long, sad howl echoing in the tower.

"Shhh." Max pulled her close and rubbed her neck even as his own heart raced.

Finally, the sounds grew softer.

"See, everything's fine." Max scanned the room.

It was clear the stones had been carved years before because some were now so weathered that Max strained to figure out what they said.

Lola kept climbing, so Max followed all the way to the third level where a recessed alcove greeted him. Above its arched stone mantle were the words:

Born beneath the wings
of the Peregrine

MOTHER MARIA ACOSTA

BABY VALENTINA

FATHER DECEASED

MOTHER ANA HERRERA

IN SWEET WAITING

FATHER MISSING

MOTHER PATRICIA ZAVALA

BABY LOURDES

FATHER UNKNOWN

"Look, Lola. These must be babies who were born in the tower, or would be born during the long journey. Poor little things. Their mothers didn't even have a cradle or a home for them. Did their fathers abandon them? Or die? Or were they the ones the mothers were running from?"

On the opposite wall, there was another alcove. Its mantle read:

The Brigade of Women

Max tried to remember what Buelo had said. *Banished . . . mistreated . . . considered less than human. We hid them . . .*

CRISTINA OLMOS

TOGETHER WITH MY SISTERS

ORALIA AND ALMA

A NEW LIFE AWAITS

MARGARITA Z

I WILL NEVER GO BACK

GOD GIVE ME STRENGTH

He spotted the word *MAÑANALAND* on one of

the stones. He pulled the rubbing from his pocket and held it out. The letters lined up.

But the rest of the stone was faint and hard to read, especially the last line, which looked as though it had been etched by a different tool, and in haste. He stepped to the side so the stone wasn't in his shadow. He could just make out the words.

RENATA ESTEBAN

MY EYES ON MAÑANALAND

my heart in Santa Maria

Renata Esteban. His mother's name . . . before she married Papá. But that didn't make sense. His mother was a guardian. And guardians were supposed to keep their identities secret. So why would she have carved her name here?

Max ran his fingers over the letters.

Maybe there was another Renata Esteban. But even as he clung to that idea, doubt clawed its way up the walls of his mind. It had to be his mother. Otherwise, why would Papá have saved the rubbing?

Was *this* what Papá and Buelo had been hiding? He shook his head, struggling to put the pieces together. He looked at all the names in the alcove. And the truth settled: His mother was once a hidden one.

She'd been part of the Brigade of Women … from Abismo. No wonder she'd been allowed to break the code and travel beyond the next guardian. The code didn't apply to hidden ones.

Murderers and thieves … cast out of their own country … shunned … spit upon … unwanted … the worst of the worst.

Is that what people would think about his mother if they found out she was a hidden one? Then the rumors about his family being guardians would come to light, too. If that happened, would some of the boys throw rocks and spit at Max and hate him? Would he and his family be driven out of their own village? Where would they go?

A wave of lightheadedness washed over him. Was he even breathing? He squeezed his eyes shut, swiping the tears as they spilled.

Lola whined and nudged him. How long had he been standing there?

He held on to her collar and let her lead him back down the stairs. In a daze, he locked the gate to the stairwell and replaced the key in its hiding spot.

The afternoon was fading. As he walked through the clearing, it started to drizzle. The wind gusted and wet bougainvillea blossoms flew from the vine, splattering the ground with red blemishes.

Max's limbs felt heavy. By the time he and Lola reached the fork, his clothes were drenched, and Lola's hair hung limp and dripping.

They were a pitiful parade, trudging along the path to the cottage with the sky weeping upon them.

Fifteen

When Max arrived at the cottage, he changed his clothes, replaced the rubbing, and stowed the box back in the closet.

By the time Buelo came through the door, whistling and carrying two market bags, Max was sitting at the kitchen table, studying ads for Volantes in a fútbol magazine. Lola slept in front of the cold hearth.

Buelo set the bags on the counter. "What is this? Lola did not greet me at the door. Is she okay?"

"I took her for a long walk," said Max. It wasn't a lie.

"After bringing her with you to unload the wood? No wonder she is tired. I am sorry I am so late. I stayed at Mariana's until the rain let up. She sent you fig jam. On the way home I ran into Miss Domínguez. She is so attentive and kind and always asks about your father. If only he would notice her. Rodrigo stopped me, too." He shook his head, frowning. "Your father called him and said there is a complication and things might take longer than he anticipated. But he has another meeting next week so that is promising."

Max went through the motions of listening while Buelo continued reporting on his day. He wanted to tell Buelo what he'd discovered, but the consequences of disobeying him and Papá—and being restricted to the cottage until Papá came home—held him back.

"Can you clean out Dulce's stall and feed her?"

When Max didn't answer, Buelo put a hand on his shoulder. "Maximiliano?"

Max looked up, his mind buzzing, his body numb. "Sorry . . . yes."

As he raked the stall, he stopped every few minutes to rub his chest, trying to erase the sense of doom that gripped him. He pitched the hay into Dulce's feed trough, and with each forkful, his resentment grew—for his mother leaving him, for Papá not taking care of the birth certificate sooner, if it could be taken care of at all. He even begrudged Buelo for his cheerfulness and pretending that everything was promising when it was clearly not. If Papá couldn't resolve his birth certificate, did Max even exist?

What was to become of him?

Max slammed the gate to Dulce's corral, and angry tears welled up. How could he carry something so enormous and troubling in his heart, yet behave as though nothing out of the ordinary had happened?

He swiped his damp cheeks. Maybe it would be easier than he thought. After all, he came from a long line of impostors, secret-keepers, and liars.

Max couldn't fool Buelo.

A few nights later at dinner, he put a hand on Max's forehead. "Are you feeling well? You are so quiet and brooding, and you have not touched your food. What is bothering you?"

"Just tired from work and practicing in the heat," he lied.

Buelo shook his head. "It seems like more than that. I think I will stay home from my card game tonight and keep an eye on you."

"No! You only play one Wednesday a month. Your friends are counting on you. I'm fine. I'll finish my dinner and clean up, then go to bed early. I promise." Max didn't want Buelo hovering. He wanted to look through Papá's box of papers one more time.

Buelo looked skeptical. "All right, then. If you are sure . . ." He put on his hat and grabbed his cane.

Max followed him outside.

It was almost sunset. The sky had an eerie yellow tinge, and a bleak blanket of clouds hovered in the east. A breeze brought a sweet grassy dampness to the air. Buelo pointed at the threatening sky. "If it storms, I will stay with Amelia and Rodrigo." Buelo patted Lola's head. "Take care of my boy, Lola." At the gate, he raised his cane to say goodbye.

Back inside, Max peered out the window and watched Buelo disappear down the path. Then he hurried to Papá's bedroom and took the box from the closet.

This time, Max carefully read each paper and laid it on the bed. He found the contract for a bridge Papá had worked on in San Clemente and rent receipts for an apartment, all around the time Max was born. At least Papá hadn't lied about living there.

There was nothing more with his mother's name on it. At the very bottom of the box, though, he found a handwritten note in a delicate, rounded script.

This is the best we can all hope for.
Please do not follow me.
I loved you. R.

R for *Renata*? This must be from his mother. How could leaving be the best they could hope for? *Loved*? Did she stop loving them?

Slowly and one by one, Max stacked the papers

back in the box to make sure he hadn't missed anything. He put the box away and shut the bedroom door behind him.

He had no appetite and gave the remainder of his supper to Lola. Raindrops began to splatter the tile roof. The sky grew dark and the wind picked up. Tree branches slapped the windows and it rained with purpose.

Max lay on the sofa.

When lightning flashed and angry thunder roared, Lola jumped up next to him. Max made space and put an arm over her. He closed his eyes and fell into a leaden sleep.

The storm lifted the roof from the cottage and the wind tore through the rooms. Max sat up, wide-eyed. Kitchen chairs and pots and pans floated above him. A great rumbling shook the walls.

On the cliff top, La Reina Gigante had uprooted and slowly traipsed toward him. The tower *was* a giant queen—the merlons and crenels became her crown; the loopholes, her eyes; the curved rock wall, her elegant skirt; and the coral tree blossoms, a fiery ruffle at her hem.

She waltzed forward through the raging weather. Hovering over Max, she plucked him from the room and held him in her arms, rocking him back and forth and singing.

Arrorró, mi niño. Arrorró, mi sol.
Arrorró, pedazo de mi corazón.
Este niño lindo ya quiere dormir;
háganle la cuna de rosa y jazmín.
Arrorró, mi niño. Arrorró, mi sol.
Duérmase, pedazo de mi corazón.

Hush, my child. Hush, my sunshine.
Hush, piece of my heart.
This beautiful child already wants to sleep;
make him a cradle of rose and jasmine.
Hush, my child. Hush, my sunshine.
Fall asleep, piece of my heart.

Those were the words he'd been struggling to remember!

La Reina Gigante gently laid Max back on the sofa and lowered her head, revealing a nest within her crown. There, in a hollow bordered by sticks and grass, the peregrine slept. La Reina softly kissed Max's forehead before standing to her full height again and swaying back toward the cliff.

"Don't leave!" called Max, scrambling after her. Through the storm's wreckage, he ran down the path to the fork and uphill, waving his arms. Breathless, he yelled, "Come back!"

His feet hammered the earth up the switch-backs, but just when he thought he'd reached the grove of coral trees, he found himself at the bottom of the hill again. "Please stay," he cried.

But La Reina Gigante moored herself back onto the cliff—once again a tower, proud and unyielding.

Even so, Max ran and ran and ran.

Sixteen

An insistent rapping woke him.

Lola leaped toward the door. Her low-throated growl confirmed that someone was on the other side. Max looked around for signs Buelo had returned. He hadn't.

Still groggy, Max glanced at the clock in the kitchen. Two in the morning! He rubbed his eyes. Who would come to the cottage at this hour? He walked to the door and leaned an ear against it. "Who's there?"

"A pilgrim, true of heart."

Max groaned. "Buelo, I'm too tired for games." He grabbed Lola's collar and opened the door.

A tall, imposing man in mud-caked boots and a jacket with many large pockets stood on the threshold. He wore an oilskin hat and gripped a walking stick in one hand.

Lola wriggled from Max's grasp, wagging her tail.

The man laughed, took off his hat, and stepped inside. He stooped to pet her. "Hello, Lola." He straightened and bowed to Max. "I am Father Romero, friend of Feliciano Córdoba Sr. and Jr. I have a . . . delivery for them. And you must be Maximiliano. I haven't seen you since before you could walk. How old are you now? Eleven?"

"Almost twelve."

Father Romero didn't wear a cassock like the priest at Our Lady of Sorrows. And Max couldn't remember hearing Papá or Buelo talk about him. But Lola seemed to trust him, and she was a good judge.

Father Romero looked over Max's shoulders. "Is your father or grandfather home?"

Max shook his head. "My father is in San Clemente. And Buelo is at a friend's."

Father Romero blew out a deep breath. "That complicates things. You see, I have a . . ." He stopped, as if something had suddenly occurred to him. "I should ask, are you familiar with . . ." He scratched his head. "How should I put this? On occasion, there are those of us who help travelers get from one place to another." He leaned forward. "Has your father or grandfather ever mentioned this?"

Was he talking about the guardians? Weren't they a thing from the past? "Do you mean the Guardians of the Hidden Ones? Yes, they've told me."

Father Romero looked relieved. "Of course they would have! So I will speak freely and in confidence. Four weeks ago, I brought a young woman here. Rosalina. Her parents had died and she was in an unfortunate situation. Your father escorted her to the next safe place. Do you recall?"

One week last month, Papá had left to work on a bridge in Valencia. Was that another lie?

Max nodded.

"Tonight, I have with me her sister, Isadora. Both have already been reported missing by the man who employed them. And there's a big reward to anyone who turns them in," said Father Romero. "People will be hungry to talk and collect. So she will need to be moved today. But your father is usually the one. Your grandfather will know what to do. I believe there are substitutes in place. I'll get her situated and stay with her until daybreak. Then unfortunately, I must leave. If you have any provisions for now, it would be helpful. Also, something to keep her warm. The tower will be drafty."

Max peered into the yard but couldn't see anyone.

"She is at the fork," said Father Romero. "And time is short."

"Yes, sorry." Max hurried into the kitchen and filled a large woven market bag with leftover bread, cheese, and a few figs. He pulled a blanket from the cupboard and grabbed one of Buelo's old sweaters. He stuffed the blanket and sweater inside the bag and set it near the door.

"Before I go, I need to point out some things on the map," said Father Romero.

Max hesitated. The only map he'd seen in their home was Papá's work map. "The one with all the bridges . . . ?"

"Yes. Quickly now."

Max started for Papá's room then stopped and turned. "Were you the one to bring my mother?"

Father Romero shook his head. "I only met her once when you were a baby. I had escorted two women to the tower. She helped me get them settled and brought you along. You were not yet walking."

Max nodded and smiled. So it *hadn't* been a dream. He had been to the ruins before.

As he hurried to retrieve the map, his mind raced. Buelo, Tío, and his aunties were no longer able to make a long journey. Who would Buelo ask to substitute? Who else could he trust? Miss Domínguez? A wild idea sprang to mind. What if *he* escorted the hidden one? He could meet the next guardian, who might have traveled with his mother. That person might know the way to Mañanaland.

He could take Lola. No one would bother them if she was along. Max had gone with Papá to remote work sites before and slept outside under the stars.

How hard could the journey be anyway, especially if his aunties and Tío and Buelo had done it?

Papá never believed Max could do anything on his own, but he could! He just needed to safely escort the hidden one and hand her off. Buelo said it only took three nights. He'd need another three nights to get back. So about a week. He'd still have plenty of time before tryouts. He could leave a note.

Max walked to the kitchen and handed Father Romero the map. "*I* will take her. I sometimes substitute for my father."

He studied Max. "I didn't realize they had already brought you into the fold." He scratched his head again. "But now that I think of it, your father was about your age when he started. Still . . ." His face twitched with worry. "This situation is fraught since we know she is being followed. Her life and yours would be in danger. We should—"

Max interrupted. "I'll take Lola. And . . ." Max stood straighter. ". . . you said she needed to be moved today. I'm pretty sure Buelo won't be back in time. And I want to do it. Guardians helped my mother. I want to do the same in return. Favor con favor se paga."

Father Romero's face softened and he smiled, his eyes crinkling. "Maximiliano, you are continuing a noble legacy. Helping someone in this way is humane and selfless."

Max stared at the floor, nodding and avoiding his eyes. If he knew the real reason Max had volunteered, he wouldn't call him selfless.

Father Romero unfolded the map on the table. "Here are my recommendations. Don't leave by way of the village road. Use the footpath behind the ruins, west of the tower. It leads to the riverbank. It's steep but well covered." He moved his finger along the river, stopping at one of the small black stars. "I'd rest at the privet thicket tonight. I think she'll be too tired for much more. And tomorrow night . . ." He skipped several stars and pointed to one farther north. "I think she could make it to the outcropping. Then depending on how things go . . ." He tapped three more markings closer to the edge of the map. "Any one of these."

Max nodded. The little black stars on the map *weren't* Buelo's fishing spots. They were places to sleep and hide.

"Follow the channel but stay away from the water's edge. You'll be too easy to spot. The river is a known path to freedom, and when someone is missing and there's a reward, people sometimes stalk the banks hoping to capture a runaway. No lights or campfires. If you're questioned, say you're headed to Caruso. Even though it's farther east than you are traveling, it's in the general direction so it won't sound suspicious."

Max nodded.

"One more thing. Stay on river right until . . ." His finger followed the river north to the last numbered circle in the far left corner. ". . . this bridge. Then cross over as usual." He tapped a spot *off* the map, on the table. "After that, you know the way."

Max bent over the map and frowned. He *didn't* know the way. Should he lie and try to convince Father Romero he'd been there but didn't remember? He touched the last circle—bridge number 38. How would he ever find what was beyond it?

"She's waiting," said Father Romero, straightening and shaking Max's hand. "Thank you, my friend. Oh, and tell your father I was happy to send the information he requested of me last week."

Father Romero quickly picked up the bag of supplies, put on his hat, and slipped into the night.

"What information?" asked Max, but he was already gone.

Max stood in the doorway for some minutes, trying to make sense of all that had just happened. He shut the door and went back to the map on the table. Now he'd have to wait for Buelo to come home and confess what he'd done. Buelo would never let Max go and would call a substitute instead.

Max scanned the legend for the corresponding name for bridge number 38.

38. The Bridge of a Thousand Mallards—wide and deep channel

Max's heart skipped as the pieces dropped into place.

He *did* know the way. He'd known it his entire life. Buelo had made sure of it.

He whispered, "In the north, far away and hidden, there is a secret bridge. It is just beyond the Bridge of a Thousand Mallards. Which makes for a lot of quacking. And after that, a dead-end cove ..."

A smile crept onto Max's face.

"Do you know what this means, Lola? It's more than a legend! It *is* a true story, just like Buelo always said. It all makes sense now. The secret bridge is the next safe place. 'A pilgrim, true of heart' is a password. And the guardabarrera is a guardian. Just like Papá, Father Romero, Buelo, Tío, my aunties, and now ..."

Max gulped at the enormity of the task before him. "... me."

TODAY

Seventeen

A breath before dawn, Max left Buelo a note and set out from the cottage, following Lola to the fork and up the switchbacks.

He adjusted the backpack he had stuffed full of provisions: another blanket, extra clothes, jam sandwiches, ham tortas—enough to feed Lola and an army—and the map wrapped in oilskin. He pulled the leather cord from beneath his shirt, letting his mother's compass dangle on the outside. If he got lost, it might help. And maybe it would make him look more credible to the hidden one, as if he'd done this before.

Above them, the peregrine swam wide loops against a watery sky. "Pilgrim bird. Traveler from a promised land," whispered Max. "Are you my mother's spirit? Or someone like her? Will you bring me good fortune and magic?" He hoped she would at least bring him safe passage.

The sun peeked out. Last night's storm had rinsed the dust from the stones at the ruins. Cobwebs glistened and the tower glowed.

He retrieved the key. "Okay, Lola, we want to give the woman fair warning and try not to alarm her."

Max pulled the outside tower door open and softly called, "Hello?"

No one answered.

Lola darted past him and rushed to the locked gate, sniffing and pawing at the rails.

Max called again, "Hello? I'm here to help." When there was no response, he unlocked the gate and climbed the stone steps with Lola pressed to his side.

Something shuffled above.

Lola charged into the stairwell and disappeared, relentlessly barking.

Max scrambled after her. "Lola!" On the fourth level, he found her, woofing deep and loud at a young girl huddled on the floor and shaking. He ran forward and grabbed Lola's collar. "I'm so sorry! Don't be scared. She won't hurt you."

The girl unfolded, still trembling, and clutched something wrapped in Buelo's old sweater. She looked just old enough for school. Her large brown eyes darted from Max to Lola and back to Max. She smoothed her blue dress. A thick fringe of hair covered her forehead and was trimmed in a straight line just above her brows. One loose braid knotted with twigs and leaves almost reached her waist. There was more dirt on her clothes and tear-streaked cheeks than on her scuffed boots. Had she been sleeping outside? She squinted and blinked several times before crouching and patting the floor until she found a pair of wire rims and put them on, making her eyes look even bigger and more frightened.

Father Romero hadn't said that the woman he was to escort was traveling with a child. Before Max could ask where she was, the bundle in the girl's arms wriggled, and a kitten peeked from the sweater.

Lola strained toward it.

"Sit!" Max commanded.

The dog whimpered but obeyed.

"This is Lola," he said. "She's harmless. She wouldn't have cornered you, except for the cat. She's a Portuguese water dog and large for her breed. But she's very gentle, at least with people. I promise."

The girl's lips quivered. Still, she said nothing.

"I'm Max. I'm the guardian. I'm here for the hidden one. Who are you?"

The girl's eyes narrowed and she backed away.

"Don't be afraid. My father was supposed to guide someone but he's away. And Father Romero said she must be moved at once." He stood taller. "I'm to say, 'I am a pilgrim, true of heart.'"

Her face relaxed a little.

Max looked around the room. "I need to talk to someone named Isadora. Do you know where she is?"

The girl swept a wisp of hair from her eyes, took a wobbly breath, and pointed to herself.

He frowned. *She* was Isadora? She was the one he

was to escort? But she was so young! How could he care for such a small child? Could she even make the journey on her spindly legs? "You're alone?"

She hugged the kitten and looked as if she might burst into tears again.

Max put both hands on his head and walked in a circle. The only little children he really knew were Chuy's sisters. All of his complaints about them echoed. They threw tantrums when they didn't get their way. They didn't do as he asked. They were loud or whiny or annoying.

The kitten mewled, interrupting his thoughts.

And why hadn't Father Romero mentioned the cat? A cat could be a problem. What if it ran off and Isadora chased it into a ravine or became hysterical? What if it meowed while they were hiding?

"I'm afraid we will have to leave the cat here."

Isadora's face wrenched and she emphatically shook her head. Tears streamed down her cheeks but she didn't make a sound.

No one had prepared him for crying! He knelt on one knee in front of her and said gently, "Please trust me. What if Lola and the kitten don't get along?"

She held out her small hand toward Lola, who inched forward, sniffing.

Within seconds, Isadora was stroking her head and neck. She set the kitten down in front of her.

Lola lowered her big body to the floor and crawled forward, nudging the kitten with her nose. It pawed at Lola's head, backed away, and pounced forward, playing. Carefully, Lola licked the kitten's back, like a mother cat.

Isadora swiped her cheeks, her eyes pleading.

Max sighed in resignation. "All right. Where are your things?"

Isadora crossed the room and started up the stone steps.

Max and Lola followed her to the top of the stairwell. There were no stones with markings this high up in the tower, except for one.

Devoted sister, Rosalina

waiting for Isadora

in Mañanaland

There was that word again, *Mañanaland*. If Isadora's sister was there, just like Max's mother, then it must be a safe haven. But where and what kind of place was it? he wondered. As if she had heard him, Isadora waved him to the landing and into the tower room.

Beneath the domed ceiling, a mural wrapped the walls. The paint was faded and cracked in some spots, but it was still a magnificent panorama. The first scene began at the landing, where a tiny church sat in the midst of burned-out buildings, street fires, and broken glass. People fled with their belongings while soldiers shot bullets over their heads.

Isadora stood in front of the scene, biting the corner of her lip.

"Abismo," whispered Max, following her to the

next section. There, a vast countryside was dotted with houses, barns, stables, and thickets, some tagged with a black silhouette of a peregrine—its head, open wings, and splayed legs like the points on a star—black stars.

Max touched one. "The sign of the falcon . . . safe places to hide."

Farther on, the wall became a tightly packed forest, every tree a person, the limbs like arms reaching for one another.

"People hiding in trees," said Max.

She closed her eyes. Her body shuddered.

What had happened to her on her journey here?

Isadora stepped aside to where the trees gave way to the citrus orchards and grape fields surrounding Santa Maria. Río Bobinado, Our Lady of Sorrows, and Max's bridge were all there, and on the cliff's edge, the tower and the ruins.

After the village, a scurry of clouds—white, purple, and gray—streaked across the wall. Lightning sprang from some, rain from others.

Then the mural burst into a lush, sunny landscape: blue skies and green hills, bougainvillea, bushes laden with berries, trees ripe with fruit, waterfalls spilling into large pools, and arcs of rainbows.

Painted above it was the word *Mañanaland*.

Isadora stopped in front of the paradise, and for the first time, Max saw a timid smile.

A swath of sunlight shined through a loophole and the room brightened. Still in awe, Max slowly turned, taking in the mural again. No wonder Tío wanted to preserve the tower.

Isadora reached out and gently touched a rainbow.

Max could feel her optimism and longing as she gazed at the beautiful scene.

Her sister was waiting for her in Mañanaland.

And hopefully, Max's mother was waiting there, too.

Eighteen

"We better get going," said Max.

The blanket he'd sent last night was spread in the middle of the room. On top of it were the left-overs of the bread and cheese and a small wooden box the size of a fist, the lid carved with an elaborate tree. Isadora picked it up and slipped it into the pocket of her dress, then stuffed the blanket and food into the market bag.

She tied the sleeves of Buelo's sweater together at the cuffs, slipped her head through the loop, and stretched the hem around her, tying the corners in a knot behind her back and fashioning a snug sling across her chest. She tucked the kitten inside.

How did she know to do such a thing?

They left the tower and descended single file down the steep, narrow path to the river, hidden between thick foliage and bottlebrush. The muddy ground sucked at their shoes. Max glanced back at

Isadora, who had already dropped behind. She had tucked her left arm into the sling, probably to pet the kitten, and used her right hand to grab branches to steady herself. He hoped she wouldn't slow him down.

When they reached the flat banks along the river, they walked north until the spire of Our Lady of Sorrows was only a speck in the distance. In the land of a hundred bridges, there were now fewer and they were much farther apart.

Max was grateful that there were no signs they'd been followed and that the weather seemed content for now. Except for the birds, the only sounds were Isadora's measured breathing, Lola's panting, and an occasional meow.

As the day dragged on, Isadora lagged farther behind, and once stopped altogether to choose a pebble from a stream. Max darted back to collect her. If she made a habit of stopping, he might never get to the guardabarrera and back home in time for tryouts!

But she didn't. After that, she kept up.

At last, by late afternoon, they came to a patch of dense privet bushes, exactly where Buelo had marked on the map. Max edged through them, holding branches aside for Isadora, until they reached a small protected spot next to the river. "We'll stay here tonight."

He spread their blankets on the ground, side by side. Then he retrieved water, put out some food for the animals, and handed Isadora a torta. He watched her pull tiny bits from the bread and ham, giving every other pinch to the kitten or Lola. "You should eat. You must be hungry and there's plenty."

Isadora shrugged. She sat on the blanket and looked upstream, rubbing her left wrist.

She still hadn't said a word. Was she afraid of him?

"You need to eat," he said gently, handing her more bread and ham. "So you can keep up your strength."

She nibbled in silence, avoiding Max's eyes.

The world around them slowly faded and turned the color of slate, until it was hard to tell where the river ended and the sky began.

In the calm of evening, Max's earlier frustrations settled. Even at Isadora's slow pace, they'd still made it to the safe spot before dark. No one appeared to be following them. And in two days' time, they'd arrive at the guardabarrera's cavern. Max could get his answers and head back home.

He sat across from Isadora. "I should tell you about the next guardian so you know what to expect."

She leaned forward.

"I've never actually met her," said Max. "But Buelo, my grandfather, told me *all* about her. I didn't believe she was real. I always thought she was just a character in a fantastic bedtime story that Buelo liked to tell." The shadows grew darker. Crickets began their songs. The slow slap of the water against the bank kept a rhythm.

Like the tinkling of glass chimes, Isadora's small voice carried. "I like stories."

Max smiled in the darkness. "Me too."

Isadora took off the sweater sling, folded it for a pillow, and put her head down next to Lola's. The kitten curled into a ball on her chest.

Max lay back on the blanket with his arms beneath his head. He imagined himself in the cottage with Buelo and could almost smell the dried rosemary in the firebox. "Far away and hidden, there is a secret bridge and a peculiar gatekeeper, a guardabarrera. Her name is Yadra. Some think she's a troll or a witch. But don't worry, it's probably not true. Buelo met her and she served him tea in a china cup. So how could she be unkind?"

Max thought about all the years Buelo had told him the story, letting it sink into his being. Had he been preparing Max to be a guardian all this time?

"More," she whispered.

"She lives beneath the bridge in a cavern. Buelo said it is very crowded because she collects so many things. You can go there if you lost something, but very few do . . ." He didn't tell Isadora everything—he left out the part about holding tomorrow in the palm of your hand—but he continued with the legend until Isadora's breathing deepened.

He pulled up the edge of the blanket, making a snug cocoon around her and the kitten. She looked even younger when she was sleeping.

Max was just about to settle himself when a branch cracked. Lola's head popped up and her ears perked. Something thudded on the ground and twigs snapped. Max froze and held his breath. Then just as suddenly, the night was silent again.

He exhaled. It was probably an animal on a nightly forage. He'd slept outside many times with Papá and there were always night noises. This had to be a safe place to sleep, he assured himself. Otherwise it wouldn't have been marked on the map.

A bright streak shot across the sky. Max could hear Chuy in his head. *A shooting star! Quick, make a wish! It will come true.*

A few weeks ago, Max would have wished to go to the fútbol clinic, or for a pair of Volantes, and to make the village team. Today his life was muddled. He wanted to meet his mother and show her that he was every bit a worthy boy. He wanted to return the compass and bring her home so Papá could stop looking and believe in happy endings again. And he wanted to retrieve proof that he was born.

If he couldn't find his mother, he could still get Isadora to the next safe place and at least prove to Papá he was capable of doing things on his own. And if the guardabarrera thought him true of heart, maybe she would take him on the journey upriver so he might hold tomorrow in the palm of his hand.

Staring into the vast sky, he felt small and insignificant. Papá wouldn't approve of wishing on a star, but Max crossed his fingers anyway. "I wish to know what will become of me and if the path I'm on is leading to a place I want to go."

Nineteen

When Max woke, the blanket was empty, and Isadora and all of her things were gone.

Max jumped up, his heart pounding. "Isadora! Lola!" Frantically, he searched the camp.

He heard a bark and followed it through the privet bushes until he spotted them upstream at river's edge. Isadora was picking wildflowers, with Lola and the kitten at her side.

He ran toward her. "Isadora, you can't disappear like that without telling me!"

Her face fell and filled with dread. She dropped the flowers, picked up the kitten, and backed away from Max, her body cowering.

He held up his hands. "No. No. I'm . . . I'm not going to hurt you. I was *worried*. I didn't know where you were." He pointed to a tree stump. "Stay there and wait for me to pack up. Please!" He hadn't meant to frighten her, but he couldn't risk losing her.

Isadora lowered herself to the stump and sat stiffly. Lola stayed at her side and hung her head, as if she was being reprimanded. Max dashed back to camp.

As he hastily stuffed his backpack, he noticed a thread of smoke downriver along the bank. Judging from the distance, the camp was hours away. Still, the idea that someone could be following dropped like a sour stone in his stomach. The more distance he put between them and whomever was on the riverbank, the better. He quickly consulted the map and then rushed back to Isadora. "Let's go."

She fell in behind him and stayed close. As the morning wore on, she had only momentary lapses when she paused to watch dragonflies or collect a feather for her pocket.

The sun burned through the clouds, but for most of the day they were able to walk in the shade of oak trees bordering the bank. By late afternoon, they came to an enormous tree lying across a stream. They'd have to cross it to stay on course.

Max climbed the end of the trunk and helped Isadora up.

But once on top, she drew back and froze, clutching the sling. She shook her head. "I . . . I can't."

Max sighed. "It's not that deep. You could probably even stand in the stream. And if you fall, I will jump in after you. So will Lola. Or you could swim. You *do* know how to swim, right?"

She nodded. "But I . . . I don't like looking down."

Impatient, he took her bag and slung it over his shoulder. "We're not that high up. Hold my hand."

She gripped his fingers.

Slowly, they sidestepped toward the middle. But then she stopped.

"Keep going," Max encouraged.

She stared into the water, taking huge breaths.

When she wobbled, he gripped her hand tighter. "Don't look down! Look at me and take a step. You can do it."

She shifted her eyes to his. He gently tugged her forward and they shuffled along the log, small step by small step. When they reached the other side, Isadora leaned against Max's chest and wrapped her arms around him. "Thank you."

Max felt his face grow warm. Awkwardly, he patted her back. "See, you did it."

Something tender spread through him. Isadora was so little, and she was trying so hard to be brave. He gave her a quick squeeze in return. "Come on. Let's find where we'll rest tonight."

The sky was growing dusky when Max came upon the enclave of boulders that Buelo had marked on the map. He hiked behind the largest to where it hollowed. "Here," he said, nodding. "This is the outcropping."

Isadora spread out the blankets while Max collected water and fed the animals.

Lola scouted the rocks. The kitten stalked a lizard, which scurried away.

When Isadora settled on the blankets, Max handed her a jam sandwich.

She took a bite, then stared at the bread, and took another bite.

"You like fig jam?" said Max.

She gave him a wobbly smile. "My mother . . ." She stopped, her eyes filling.

Softly Max said, "Your mother used to make it?"

She nodded. "Every year. Then we gave a jar to each of the neighbors. My papi said the best gifts are the ones you make with your own hands. He liked to make things with wood." She pulled the box from her pocket and traced the carving on the lid. "He made this. It's our fig tree."

Max chimed in, with the hope Isadora would keep sharing too. "Buelo has two sisters, Amelia and Mariana. They are my great aunts but more like grandmothers. Mariana has a fig tree, too, and I used to help her make jam. I peeled and smashed the figs. That was my favorite part. When it was time to cook, she brought a chair to the stove and let me stand on it."

Isadora's eyes brightened. "My mami did that, too."

"Mariana put her hands over mine and we both held the wooden spoon and stirred the figs," said Max. "The kitchen smelled warm and sugary . . ."

Isadora whispered. "Mamá tied my hair back . . ."

Her voice was so soft Max had to lean forward to hear.

"The steam made my hair all curly. Rosalina called me frizzy-head. Mamá put a little warm jam in a bowl and let me eat it."

"Mariana did the same!" said Max, remembering the cozy kitchen, and how he'd carefully carried the glass jar of fig jam home to show Buelo and Papá.

The kitten proudly deposited the lizard's tail on the blanket as an offering.

Max petted his head. "You're a good hunter." He looked at Isadora. "Did you name him?"

She nodded. "Churro. When my mami was a little girl, she had a cat this same color named Churro."

He was the color of fried dough rolled in cinnamon and sugar. "It suits him," said Max.

She lay down on the blanket with the kitten and rubbed her wrist.

"Isadora, did you hurt yourself?" he asked.

But she closed her eyes and didn't answer.

Had he gripped her too tightly when they'd crossed the log earlier? He hoped not.

The sky grew dark, but the moon was out in force. Max waited until Isadora was asleep and climbed the large boulder, using the ones around it as stepping stones. From the flat top, he could see for miles. The water was shallower here and licked over the river rocks, sounding like a persistent rain.

His eyes swept across the horizon downriver and spotted the bright glow of a campfire.

Someone *was* following.

Twenty

Max slept fitfully, dreaming of pursuers who stalked the banks with fire torches and guns.

Before the sun rose, his eyes flew open and he sat up, his breathing fast and shallow.

A light mist covered the river. The world was gray and quiet. It was early, but he was eager to get moving. He roused Isadora, and after sharing another jam sandwich, they were on the move. Max's thoughts were on tomorrow, when they'd finally reach the guardabarrera. He walked quickly, and Isadora kept pace.

By noon, they arrived at a bridge and found the wing walls overrun with ripe blackberries. Max and Isadora fell upon them, stuffing their mouths and tossing handfuls to Lola. Soon, their bellies were full and their hands stained purple. Churro could not be convinced to eat even one.

Max and Isadora washed their hands and faces

in the river. Lola bounded from beneath the bushes and joined them at the water's edge.

"Ewww, Lola! What did you get into? You smell awful!" Max complained.

Isadora held her nose.

"She must have rolled in animal scat." Max coughed and waved a hand in front of his face. They couldn't keep going with her smelling like that.

He picked up a stick and threw it into the river away from the bridge. "Lola, go!"

Lola sprang into the water and landed with a splash, legs churning and head straining toward the floating stick. When she returned, Max threw the stick farther out. "Once more, Lola. Then you'll be tolerable."

Isadora giggled.

"She loves to swim," said Max. "That's why fishermen keep her breed on their boats. She will fetch anything in the water. I just have to give the command."

A voice yelled from behind them, "You there! You children! Who's that in the river?"

Max and Isadora spun around.

On the bridge's deck, a man leaned over the capstones almost directly above them. He held a rifle. "I was parked in the shade eating my lunch and I heard a splash. Is everyone okay?"

Max noticed a battered green truck parked beneath a large oak on the other side of the bridge. His stomach wrenched. Why hadn't he remembered to stay off the river? "It's just our dog. She likes to swim," called Max.

The man stared at them, then looked around. "What are you two doing out here?"

"We . . . we're on our way to our aunt's house," said Max. "In Caruso."

The man shook his head. "You must be lost. I'm from a village an hour north, and I'm heading to one another hour south, and that's driving, not on foot. There's nothing in between. Caruso is hours away, after you cross the next bridge and then due east."

"We know the way," called Max.

"Is that right?" He put his hands on his hips and tilted his head as if questioning Max's answer. "Well, I heard this morning that the police are looking for two missing girls," said the man. "Big reward, too. Have you seen them?"

Isadora shrank behind Max.

"No," said Max, shaking his head. "We haven't seen anyone."

The man rubbed his chin. "You two better come with me. It's not safe to be wandering out here alone. I'll take you to the nearest police station. They can call your aunt to come get you."

Lola ran onto the bank, dripping from the river and carrying the stick in her chops when she noticed the man. Her growl simmered. Max quickly clipped the leash to her collar and slipped on his backpack. He picked up Isadora's bag and whispered, "Just follow me. Can you keep up?"

Isadora clutched the sling and nodded.

"Thank you," called Max. "We'll be right up."

The man waved and walked toward the truck.

As soon as he turned his back, Max, Isadora, and Lola darted through the bridge's tunnel and along the opposite bank.

They could hear the man yelling, "Wait! Stop! I'm reporting you!"

But they never looked back. They ran until they were gulping air.

Max scrambled up a steep hill to the top of the ridge, Lola panting at his side. Isadora struggled after them, slipping on the loose rocks every few steps and once falling to her knees when a foothold gave way.

Max helped her over the top, where they crouched to catch their breath.

Isadora's dress was torn, her legs were scraped, and her entire body shook. She clung to his arm.

Gathering his courage, Max peeked over the crest, hoping he wouldn't be looking down the barrel of a rifle.

Twenty · One

The truck sped down the bridge road, away from them.

"He's gone." Max felt the tension seep from his body.

Tears spilled down Isadora's dusty cheeks, leaving muddy tracks. "I can't go back . . . I can't . . ."

"Listen. It's going to take that man at least an hour to get to the next village. He will need time to talk to the police. Then it would take another hour to return to this spot. That's two hours, probably more. We'll be far upriver by then. And at the hidden bridge tomorrow morning. But we have to get moving."

Isadora's sobs seemed to root her in place.

How did Chuy console his sisters? Sometimes he bribed them with ice cream or candy, or told them a joke, or promised to show them something they'd never seen before.

"Arrorró. Arrorró. Shhh. Shhhh," said Max.

"You know, Isadora, *I* want to get to the next safe place, too. And do you know why? Because I have a big secret."

He held out a hand and she took it, letting him help her up. "Let's walk, and I will tell you something I've never told anyone before."

She took a shaky breath. "Not even your best friend?"

Max shook his head. "Not even my best friend. Do you want me to tell you about him?"

She wiped her face with her hem and nodded.

"His name is Chuy." Max talked fast—about how Chuy buzzed his hair, his little sisters, the water hole, and their fútbol dreams. The memories flooded Max with something rich and sweet, like leche quemada. Then Max remembered what he'd said to Chuy, about being like a stray dog. He wished he could take back those words and hoped Chuy would forgive him. "See, you have Rosalina. But I never had a sister or a brother—someone with almost all the same memories. The closest I have is Chuy."

"Then why doesn't he know the secret?" she asked.

Max paused. Why hadn't he told Chuy? He could trust him not to tell. Why had he wasted time being jealous and angry? "I will tell him when I get home. But I'll tell you first."

"Are you running away?" she asked. "Do you live with someone awful who scares you?"

"No! Papá is kind. And so is Buelo. They love me very much. So does Tío. And my aunties. They all love me."

Isadora looked at him with her big, earnest eyes. "You're lucky."

Max felt a pang in his chest, for everything he had that Isadora didn't. Suddenly, his problems felt small.

"What is the secret?" she asked.

Max hesitated. Should he tell her? Maybe it would make her feel better, knowing his mother was from Abismo, too, and that he had struggles, in spite of all the good things in his life.

"My mother was a hidden one."

"Like me and Rosalina?"

Max nodded. "She left when I was a baby." He lifted the compass. "This was hers. Her mother gave it to her."

"So she would always know the way," said Isadora.

Max smiled. "Maybe. She lost it and Papá found it after she left. He gave it to me. I want to talk to the guardabarrera to see if she knows how I can find my mother in Mañanaland . . ."

Once Max started talking, he couldn't seem to stop. He told Isadora the rest—about the papers his mother took and how she stole a piece of Papá's spirit and that he wanted to know what was to become of him.

Isadora squeezed Max's hand. "The guardabarrera will know how to find her."

"Yes," said Max. "I'm counting on that."

For the rest of the afternoon, Max pretended to stay focused on the route, but inside he was jittery.

In this remote area, there were no footbridges, and the spans were all connected by roads, which meant trucks and cars could pass. He kept looking for the man in the green truck, trying hard not to let Isadora sense his anxiety.

When they stopped for a short break, he pulled out the map and studied it again, making sure they stayed away from the roads as much as possible. He glanced at Isadora, who was leaning against a tree, eyes closed, her tiny hands petting Churro. How far could she travel today before she was too tired to go on? Or before it grew dark? The weight of what he'd undertaken pressed in on him.

Isadora kept up, stoic and determined. By dusk, they had made it to the resting place marked on the map, beneath the canopy of a giant willow tree near the river.

They settled for their last night, Lola between them, as always. Thick low limbs splayed above them, and thin leafy branches dipped toward the ground like draperies, hiding them from the world.

Isadora examined the tear in her dress. "I could fix it, if I had better light."

"You can sew?" Max exclaimed. She was so little.

She pulled the wooden box from her pocket and opened it. Inside were a pair of mending scissors, a few needles, thread, a handful of buttons, and a thimble. Her voice was soft. "Mami taught us. My seams aren't as straight as Rosalina's yet. But someday I'll be a good seamstress. At night while we sewed, my papi worked on his carvings and told us stories. I always begged for one more story."

"No wonder you like stories," said Max.

"My mother made curtains at the factory and my father fixed the machines. They worked long hours. It was a sad place. Then after . . . me and Rosalina, we didn't have any place to go."

"You mean after your parents died?" asked Max.

"Yes." At first, Isadora talked slowly, as if the words were steep mountains she had to climb. "The police said we could stay together if we cleaned house for a very important man. He promised to let us go to school. But he never did. I begged every day. He didn't like that. One day he grabbed my hand to make me stop asking . . . and twisted it." She winced. "It broke."

Max's stomach turned. Poor Isadora.

Her breathing quickened, and her words spewed. "Rosalina called the doctor. But he couldn't put a cast on until it wasn't swollen anymore. He made me a sling from a sweater and asked me how did it happen? The important man did not want me to talk. I told anyway. And he was very angry. He said I was lying." Her eyes pleaded. "I wasn't. I promise." She chewed on her bottom lip.

"I believe you," said Max.

Isadora sat up and leaned forward. "The doctor whispered to us that the man wanted to *marry* Rosalina when she turned fourteen. That was only in a few weeks! Rosalina started to cry. The doctor said someone would come and help us soon."

"Did someone come?" asked Max.

"Yes. The next day the cook came from the

church and said the priests needed us to sew vestments because they heard we were good with the needle. *He* said I couldn't sew, but the cook said I could do hoop work with one hand and it was very important church business. She took us to the house next to the chapel. But I never sewed anything. A guardian came that night to take Rosalina. I begged to go, too, but the doctor wouldn't let me until he put a cast on my arm. For a month, I couldn't do much except pick flowers from the garden and arrange them for the church. Every night I cried for Rosalina. But I didn't make any noise. The cook said it was fine to cry but I had to do it silently so I wouldn't be found."

"Did the man ever come looking for you?"

"Two times he came and the cook told him to go away because there was still sewing to do. Then he came again and was very angry. He yelled that he was coming back to get us the next Saturday. He didn't know Rosalina was already gone. The next night the doctor cut off my cast and took me to a safe place."

"What was the cook going to say when the man returned?"

"That we disappeared."

"You must have been so scared," said Max.

"I wasn't scared of leaving. I was scared of staying . . . and of the man."

Isadora lay down and gazed into the branches. "This is a good tree. We hid in trees."

Max thought back to the mural on the wall of the tower. "When you were running away?"

She nodded. "People searched for runaways in the forest. The guardian saw them coming so we climbed high in the branches and held on tight. We couldn't make a sound. The searchers walked right underneath us. I tried not to look down. I didn't even blink my eyes. After we were safe, though, I couldn't stop shaking and crying."

Max's throat tightened and he choked out his words. "Isadora, you are the bravest person I know,"

The evening grew darker. Isadora yawned. "After the forest, Father Romero came for me." She pulled the kitten closer. "I found Churro on the way to the beautiful tower. I wish I had scratched my name on the wall next to Rosalina's. To show I made it that far."

The leaves shushed above them. River water trickled. Far away, a nightingale sang.

"I will put your name there," said Max. "I promise."

Eyes closed, she whispered, "Thank you."

Max stared into the night, unable to settle. What horrible fate would Isadora face if she was caught and taken back to Abismo? Worry squeezed him. Something fierce and expansive mushroomed inside him—something bigger than his search for his mother—like enormous protective wings, beating with the resolve to deliver Isadora to safety.

No matter what.

Twenty · Two

The Bridge of a Thousand Mallards was made from the palest red stones.

Its three arches and their mirror images on the water created a chain of rose-colored globes. In the morning sun, it looked like a passage to a magical land.

The bridge was only about fifteen feet at the keystone, with a bench below the parapet and wide capstones. A deep, lazy channel stretched below it. There was no doubt how it received its name. Rafts of ducks paddled in the water and huddled on the grassy knolls surrounding the banks. Lola dashed back and forth to the river's edge, whining and begging to retrieve. Max clipped her to the leash, but still the ducks erupted into the air, quacking and rasping.

They'd be safe once they crossed the bridge and hiked a little farther. But Max couldn't relax. Earlier he'd thought he might have heard a motor, but then the sound disappeared. Had he just imagined it? His eyes dashed from one bank to the other.

He was relieved to finally spot the cove.

Max pointed upstream and across the channel to the far bank on river left. "Look, Isadora! That's where we're going." The bank was overgrown and dense, so it would take a while to reach the inlet. Buelo had said it was only another hour to the secret bridge and the guardabarrera.

Max grabbed Isadora's hand and they hurried to cross the cobbled deck. But when they reached the center, Lola growled and would not move.

Max looked around. He didn't see or hear anything. "What is it, girl?"

Lola planted her legs and snarled. That's when Max saw the green truck from yesterday slowly inching across the end of the bridge, blocking their way. The man parked and climbed from the cab, holding the rifle at his side.

Isadora clung to Max, who could barely contain Lola. She barked wildly and tried to charge.

"Better settle that dog!" called the man.

Max cried out, "Lola, sit!"

The man took a few steps toward them. "I checked with the police. She is one of the missing girls and there's a hefty reward for her. Anybody heading to Caruso has to cross this bridge, and I knew the ducks would send up an alarm as soon as you set foot on it. Don't think about running this time. I have someone waiting on the other side." He nodded toward the end of the bridge.

Max spun around. A police officer stood at the deck's entrance. Behind him, the bumper of his car showed through the thicket of trees and bushes.

"All we want is the girl," called the man.

Isadora trembled. "No . . ."

Max's body tensed. What could he do? Regret showered him. He should never have pretended he was Papá's substitute. Father Romero had warned that their lives would be in danger. And yet, he had foolishly undertaken the journey anyway, for his own selfish reasons. How could he ever have thought himself capable of being responsible for another person's life? How could he possibly hand her over?

Isadora whimpered. "Please don't let him take me."

Fear for Isadora gripped him. He managed to put an arm around her and call to the man. "Don't come any closer. You're scaring her. Let me . . . let me tell her goodbye."

The man nodded. "Make it quick. Then send her over to the truck."

Max knelt on one knee in front of Isadora so they were eye to eye.

He squeezed his hands into fists so they wouldn't shake. "I'm sorry, Isadora. I didn't want it to end like this. Please forgive me."

Her chest heaved and tears rolled down her cheeks.

It was all Max could do not to cry, too. "I'll fig-ure something out. I will follow him. *I will find you.* I promise." But even as he said it, Max knew that was impossible. The man had a truck, and Max was on foot.

"I d-don't want to l-leave you," she stammered.

Max looked at either end of the deck. He couldn't see a way out.

A guardian had to be ready to improvise at a moment's notice.

"No matter what," he whispered. He grabbed her hand. "I have an idea. But you must be the bravest you've ever been. Give me Churro and your glasses and your sewing box. And take off the sling."

Her lips quivered.

"Trust me," he whispered.

Sobbing and hiccupping, she did what he asked.

Max pulled the backpack to the front of his body. He tucked the glasses and the wooden box in the smaller pockets. He stuffed the sling in the bot-tom of the large pocket, and put the kitten on top.

"Leave the bag here. There's nothing in it we need."

Isadora looked toward the man at one end of the deck and to the police officer at the other. She choked out her words. "Which . . . way . . . should . . . I go?"

"Neither," whispered Max. "Just do as I say. We're going to take a shortcut."

Max unclipped Lola, ordered her to stay, and stuffed the leash into his pocket. He pulled Isadora up onto the stone bench and then to the capstones. "Don't look down. Look at me. This is our chance. Do you understand?" He locked eyes with her.

She nodded and bit her lip so hard that blood pearled up.

When the men saw what Max and Isadora meant to do, they ran toward them, waving and yelling. But it was too late.

Max and Isadora jumped.

Twenty · Three

The plunge was cold and the water churned around them. Through bubbles, Max saw Isadora's face, her cheeks puffing out as she held her breath. Her dress ballooned. He motioned for her to kick her legs, and they broke the surface at the same time, gasping.

Max opened the flap on the backpack and Churro sprang from it, clawing at Max's neck and head. He grabbed the kitten by the nape and held him above the water.

The men tried to get close to their jumping-off point, but Lola barked and growled, keeping them back.

Max took a few strokes away from the bridge. "Lola, come!"

She leaped from the capstones. As she splashed into the river, every duck on the water lifted into the air. Lola paddled toward Max and Isadora.

Isadora bobbed lower, her eyes filled with fear. "Churro!" she screamed.

Max quickly pushed Churro toward Lola. The kitten swam frantically until Lola grasped him by the nape, like a mother cat.

Max yelled, "He's safe. Isadora, kick your legs!"

She rose higher in the water and swam toward Max.

He grabbed her hand. Together they moved themselves through the river until Isadora could reach Lola's collar. She hung on, with Max side-stroking next to her.

By the time the men reached the middle of the deck and leaned over the capstones, Lola was already ferrying the little brigade up the middle of the river, making fast time in the glassy water. Max knew they wouldn't shoot. They couldn't risk hitting Isadora. To claim the reward, they had to bring her back alive.

Max surveyed the land on the other side. Thankfully, there were no roads anywhere that he could see, and the bank was far too overgrown for any vehicle to pass. But when he glanced back, he spotted the men hiking down the bridge's revetment toward the riverbank, on the same side of the river to which Max and Isadora were headed.

They slogged out of the water onto the narrow beach. The men were no longer in sight, but they couldn't be far behind.

Isadora shook uncontrollably, her teeth chattering. Max put Churro in her arms and her eyeglasses on her face.

"You did it, Isadora! I'm so proud of you. But we need to keep going a little farther." Max held her arm as they walked north, leading her through dense shrubbery to keep out of sight.

"Are they c-coming?" asked Isadora.

"We are a good distance ahead of them, but we have to walk as fast as we can until we reach the cove."

Within the leafy bushes, Max could no longer see the shore. They pressed on but still couldn't find the inlet. From the bridge, it had been easy to spot, but now Max was disoriented. Had they gone too far and missed it?

"Isadora, stop. We need to find the river. Listen for the trickling."

Isadora's eyes filled with anxiety. "Are we lost?"

Lola whined and Max shushed her.

"I just need to get my bearings. We need to go north. That I know for sure." Max slipped the compass from his neck. He placed it in the palm of his hand until the needle swept toward the *N*.

"Okay, follow me. It can't be much farther." He hoped he was right. What if he'd gone too far and missed the cove entirely? If he didn't find it today, they'd have to hide, then try to double back tomorrow. Max could see Isadora was tired but he had to keep them moving.

When she slowed, he took her hand and gently pulled her forward. "We can't give up now, Isadora. Come on . . . you can do it."

Lola suddenly bounded forward into the bushes and disappeared.

"Lola!" Max called, groaning. He called her again. When she didn't return, he pushed aside the thick foliage and found himself on a narrow beach where the shore curved. The cove!

They caught up to Lola and saw what looked like a dead end. But at the back of the curve, vines and willows arched across the water, creating a thick veil. Max shoved aside branches to find the unmistakable stonework of the secret bridge.

He inched toward the center, separating the tangle until he found an opening. They ducked into the bridge's shadowy underbelly and followed a narrow stone walkway that hugged the tunnel wall. *If you weren't searching for this, you would never find it*, thought Max.

They came to a wooden door with a black iron knocker—a peregrine with a ring in its talons.

Twenty · Four

Max lifted the ring and rapped the plate four times.

"I hear footsteps," Isadora whispered.

Someone called out, "Who stands before me?"

Max tried to slow his breathing. "A pilgrim, true of heart."

The door popped open.

A woman much taller than Papá or Buelo faced them. She was broad shouldered with rosy cheeks and a wide smile. Her long silver hair was tied in a tail that draped over her shoulder. She wore a plaid blouse and a printed apron over a skirt that came to the tops of her large, incompatible boots, one blue, and the other yellow. If people were to see her imposing figure lumbering along the banks at night, Max understood why they might think she was a troll. Or a river witch.

She looked at Max as though waiting for him to announce himself.

He straightened his shoulders. "I am Maximiliano Feliciano Esteban Córdoba, son of Feliciano Córdoba Jr. and grandson of Feliciano Córdoba Sr. And this is Isadora, who is traveling to meet her sister, Rosalina."

Lola sniffed the woman's boots and wagged her tail.

"That's Lola," said Max. He pointed to the kitten. "And Churro."

"And I am Yadra, nothing more, nothing less." She rummaged in her apron pocket, pulled out a handkerchief, and gently blotted Isadora's face, dabbing away the blood on her lip. "Isadora, your sister is waiting at the next safe place so that you may travel on together." She looked at Max. "Were you followed?"

"Yes," he said gravely. "To the bridge with all the ducks. We jumped in the river and Lola swam us across. Two men are looking for us."

Yadra pulled them inside and bolted the door. "They won't find you here. But the sooner I move her, the better."

Isadora gazed up at Yadra as if she were an angel. "We thought you would be . . . different."

"A troll? Or a witch?" said Yadra. "I've heard what they say. It's been the same my entire life. Everyone *thinks* they know who I am, even if we've never met." She put an arm around Isadora. "Come. Let's get you two into some clean clothes and then I'll give you something to eat and drink."

As they followed Yadra down a flight of stone steps, Max suddenly realized how tired and thirsty he was. The enormity of the past few days settled on him. Were they safe now?

Lanterns on the rock walls flickered. The yeasty smell of baked bread wafted into the stairwell. Lola pushed past them and darted ahead.

"Oh my, one of us is hungry," said Yadra, laughing. "Did I mention I love visitors and dogs?" She reached out and petted Churro. "And kittens, too, of course.

"Now, when we get into the cavern, don't be alarmed," said Yadra. "It might seem a bit overwhelming at first. I like to call it my garden of the miscellaneous."

At the bottom of the stairs, towers of folded blankets and tablecloths hugged the walls. Large metal bins held boat oars. Glass jars, still labeled with the former contents—pickled eggs, fig jam, pigs' feet—had been stacked in gleaming pyramids. Baskets lined both sides of a long hallway.

"Where did it all come from?" asked Max, amazed.

"They are left-behinds. People on a journey sometimes discard the unnecessary," said Yadra. "Or pass-alongs from the generous river. Because of the currents, anything the river swallows upstream often ends up downstream trapped in my cove. I collect it and pass it along to those in need. Once a year, everything goes to a home for women and children, and then I start collecting all over again."

Yadra took Isadora's hand and led them around an old rowboat filled with gloves and socks without mates. She reached in and grabbed two socks, one red and the other striped, and handed them to Isadora.

They stopped in front of a row of giant baskets. After studying them for size, Yadra pulled out clean shorts and a shirt for Max, and a soft purple dress for Isadora, and sent them to separate nooks to change.

They followed Yadra to a large stone kitchen, where the sun streamed in from a small window far above, and a loaf of bread cooled on the back of the stove. "Please, sit," she said, directing them to the table. She hummed and put the kettle on for tea. Max couldn't keep his eyes off of Yadra's shimmery hair and odd clothes, or her wide smile that seemed to make the room brighter. She clucked and fussed over them, reminding Max of Mariana and Amelia.

Yadra brought the kettle to the table and placed the bread on a board with a round of cheese and sliced it, encouraging them to eat. Still humming, she fixed bowls of food for the animals.

Isadora looked around. "Do you live here all by yourself?"

"Not always," said Yadra. "But I keep to myself. I was once a hidden one, like you. No one can hurt me now, but the fear of being discovered runs very deep."

"You ran away from Abismo, too?" asked Isadora.

Yadra shook her head. "I didn't run away from another country. Cruelty doesn't only happen across borders. Unfortunately, it happens everywhere, even in our own backyards."

"What do you mean?" asked Max.

"My father and mother were very strict about how I should live my life."

Max nodded. He knew how that felt. He couldn't even take a bus to Santa Inés with his friends.

"When I grew into a young woman and was old enough to make my own decisions, my parents were not pleased with my choices. And when I did not comply with their idea of me, I became invisible to them. My own parents did not see *me*. They only saw their own disappointment. They could not accept the living, breathing human standing before them, needing their love."

That wasn't like Papá or Buelo at all. They loved Max. But what would it be like when his friends and other people found out his mother was a hidden one? Would they be cruel? Would he become invisible too?

"They hurt your feelings," said Isadora.

"That must have been a hard time," said Max.

Yadra nodded. "Thankfully, others saw me and recognized I needed help. Guardians helped me figure out who I was and where I would fit into the world. One of them told me I didn't have to endure hardship by myself. Isn't that the most comforting thought—that there is always someone to help and you don't ever have to struggle alone?"

Isadora slipped from her chair and hugged

Yadra. Max blinked back tears. Yadra was so honest and so easily shared her secrets—the sad ones and the hopeful ones. He wanted to be like that.

"There, there, both of you," said Yadra, sending Isadora back to her chair. "Enough about me. Maximiliano, I have heard so much about *you*. And here you are. You're very young to be one of us. Then again, you've been nurtured by guardians. It runs in the family."

Max couldn't lie to Yadra. "They don't know I'm here. My father and grandfather weren't home when the guardian came with Isadora. I tricked him and said I sometimes substitute for my father, but I don't. This is my first time. I left a note so Buelo would know where I am, but I'm sure he is still worried."

"I will let them know that you were a worthy guardian and proved yourself. I'm very impressed you managed this all on your own. You are a courageous and selfless young man to risk your life for another."

Max shook his head. "I'm *not* courageous and selfless . . . I came for my own reasons."

Yadra raised an eyebrow.

"Buelo told me once that you could help find things and answers to perplexing questions."

"Sometimes, yes."

Isadora whispered, "He wants to find his mother and make his papá happy again."

Yadra sighed. "Well, I'm afraid that is problematic."

"But, you met her, right?" said Max. "And took her to the next safe place? She must have told you something . . ."

Yadra nodded. "I met her, of course. It's easy to see you are her son with those eyes."

He held out the compass. "She lost this and it meant something to her. I thought I could return it. And meet her . . . and see if maybe she'd come home . . ."

Yadra leaned her head back and closed her eyes. When she opened them, she said, "You see,

Maximiliano, not *everything* is findable. The road of life is littered with lost things—papers, people, answers, the other half of a pair . . . the truth. And remnants of someone's happiness can't always be recovered."

"But she's in Mañanaland. And that's the same place you're taking Isadora, right?"

Yadra smiled but looked confused. "Well . . . yes. But—"

"Can I go there with you?" blurted Max. "To take Isadora and find my mother? Please?"

Yadra slowly poured more tea in their cups. "I sense you are motivated by goodness, Maximiliano, and that your heart is true. But it is a difficult journey with hours of rowing . . ."

"I could help. I'm a good rower," said Max.

"I want him to come," said Isadora.

Yadra looked from Isadora to Max. "What about Lola? There's not much room in the boat, and I couldn't risk her barking."

"She could stay here," said Max. "We could leave

food and water and make a bed for her. She'd be fine."

Yadra's mouth twitched. "You know I could not allow you to go any farther than the next guardian. There's a—"

"A code. I know," said Max.

She studied him. "Please understand that you may find nothing you are expecting and everything unforeseen."

Max didn't understand, but he nodded anyway.

Twenty · Five

In the early evening, Yadra combed and braided Isadora's hair and tied purple ribbons at the ends. She brought piles of blankets to the kitchen and made soft beds on the floor. "You both need to rest now. We must leave in the middle of the night. I'll wake you when it's time."

Lola and Churro curled up together between Max and Isadora.

"Are you excited?" whispered Max.

"Yes," said Isadora. "But I wish you could come with me even *after* tomorrow."

"You'll have Rosalina. And there will be a guardian. You won't be alone." He hoped it was true. He hoped she'd always have someone to protect her.

"Besides," he teased. "You'll forget me soon enough."

"No, I won't! Not ever!"

He smiled. "Maybe someday, when I'm a famous

footballer . . . you will find me and come to see me play."

"I *will* find you," said Isadora.

Even though it wasn't likely, imagining it made Max happy.

It was dark and cozy in the cavern. Lola moaned in her sleep. Max thought Isadora had drifted off, too, until she said, "One more story?"

He was glad to keep talking. "Once upon a time, there was a little girl who was very tired but could not go to sleep. Every time her eyes closed, they popped opened again, like a caja sorpresa. It was only after she heard a magical song that she was finally able to slumber." He sang, *"Arrorró, mi niño. Arrorró, mi sol. Arrorró, pedazo de mi corazón . . ."*

She continued. *"Este niño lindo ya quiere dormir, háganle la cuna de rosa y jazmín."*

"You know this song?" asked Max.

Isadora yawned and murmured, "All mothers sing it to their children. My mother sang it to me . . . and her mother sang it to her . . ."

Was that why he remembered it? Somewhere long ago and far away, had his mother sung it to him?

Max hummed the song, softer and slower until Isadora was asleep.

Buelo was right. It was going to be hard to say goodbye.

TOMORROW

Twenty · Six

The sky was mottled with dark clouds that almost eclipsed the moonlight. The river was black ink.

They had left well before dawn in the small boat. Yadra sat in back, deftly rowing, Max on the front thwart opposite, watching the river recede. Isadora snuggled into him and slept, with Churro tucked in a new sling.

As the river grew straight and wide, time stretched and Max's mind drifted. He had no sense of how long he'd been gone. He had to think hard about what day it was. Monday.

Tomorrow it would be exactly three weeks since Papá had left for San Clemente. That meant yesterday would have been Sunday dinner. He pictured Amelia sitting beneath the oak tree at the cottage, working in her puzzle book, Buelo cooking in the kitchen with Mariana, and Papá and Tío playing chess at the old picnic table. He wondered if Chuy had come looking for him to go to the water hole. Santa Maria and everyone in his life felt so far away. Even the fútbol tryouts seemed distant and oddly unimportant.

As if reading his mind, Yadra said, "You must miss home. I can see you are carrying many burdens of your own. Even though you have come seeking answers for yourself, you *have* been brave and selfless. You never left Isadora, and you risked your own life to save hers. Your father and grandfather will be proud of you."

Max let the words sink in. "I hope so." Would they be angry when they discovered he'd disobeyed them?

"Isadora has grown attached to you, and you to her," said Yadra.

Max nodded in the darkness. He tried not to think about the return trip without her. "Do she and her sister have any other family to take care of them? Someone waiting in Mañanaland?"

Yadra kept her voice low. "Their parents were killed by military police while protesting conditions in the factory where they worked. As far as I know, there is no one else."

"Her sister is only two years older than I am. How will they live?"

"The guardians won't abandon them. The network is wide and deep."

Max repositioned Isadora so that she was snug in the crook of his arm. She was lucky that there was a place like Mañanaland where, unlike Santa Maria, everyone was welcome. "Is Mañanaland a big country or a small one? When we arrive, is there someone I can ask about my mother?"

Yadra stopped rowing. "Maximiliano, I don't think you understand. Mañanaland is not a destination. It's a . . . way of thinking."

He frowned. What did that mean? "But, isn't that where we are going?"

"In a sense, yes. We're taking Isadora to the next guardian. Then she and Rosalina will go on to somewhere else so that they might leave a painful past behind and have a new life with at least the possibility of happiness. Where they, or any hidden one for that matter, end up could be anyplace and will remain unknown to me . . . and to you."

"But . . . my mother carved on a stone that her eyes were on Mañanaland. And Isadora's sister said she was waiting in Mañanaland."

"Your mother's eyes were on a hope and dream," said Yadra. "And Rosalina meant that she was waiting for her sister somewhere safe where they could live without fear of whatever happened in Abismo. After you've experienced a terrifying and anguished existence, anywhere better . . . is Mañanaland."

Max felt his face flush. All this time he had foolishly hoped to find a place when none existed? He struggled to make sense of it. "But . . . then . . . where did you take my mother?"

"To the next guardian."

"Can I ask *her* or *him* about my mother?"

Yadra shook her head. "That guardian moved away long ago. And I've never had occasion to assist on the next leg of the journey, so *I* don't even know where the hidden ones go after I hand them off. I only know that they travel by train."

"Did . . . did my mother tell you *anything* about why she left?"

"I had to move her quickly, just like Isadora. She was with two other young women so we didn't have the chance to talk privately. At first, she posed as the guardian but then admitted she had been a hidden one and needed to move on. She said it was for the safety of her family. I told your father the same years ago when he came searching for her. She was brave and determined and risked her own life to guide the two women here, even if it was also for herself. You are like her in that way."

Max let Yadra's words sink in. "But you have to know *something* more. I came all this way, and Buelo said you'd have answers."

"I'm sorry, Max. That's all I know."

Max's body deflated from the weight of her words. Without any more clues, how would he ever find his mother? Or know what his own future held? Maybe

Papá was right not to believe in happy endings.

Yadra continued to row.

Max turned his head away from her and silently wept.

By midmorning, rain threatened. The landscape turned to rolling hills with few trees. Max and Yadra took turns rowing and resting. After what felt like hours, Yadra slowed the boat and searched the riverbank.

"What are you looking for?" asked Max.

"A signal," said Yadra.

A lone cottage near the top of a hill came into view. "Look for smoke from the chimney."

Within minutes, a plume rose from the bricks.

Yadra pulled the oars and moved the boat upstream again. "That was the sign that it's safe to proceed. Señorita Villa will meet us."

"Is she the next guardian?" asked Max.

"Yes. She is new, like you, but not quite as young. She has already helped many women find their way."

Within minutes, they had tied the rowboat to a small, isolated pier and waited under a large oak near the riverbank. Isadora clutched Max's hand.

Yadra searched the horizon until a car threaded through the foothills and rattled toward them. When it stopped, two women emerged.

Isadora dropped Max's hand, took a few steps forward, and then flew into her sister's arms. For a moment there was no sound, except muffled crying and then quiet laughter. He couldn't tell who clung to the other more tightly.

Yadra put an arm around his shoulder. "We don't often get to see reunions. We usually just send people off toward the horizon. This makes it worth it, yes?"

Max swiped at his eyes and nodded.

Señorita Villa was barely taller than Max and didn't look much older than Rosalina. With her hair beneath a bandana and a smock apron over her clothes, she looked like any young woman who might work in a market stall. She embraced Yadra and then the two women stepped aside to talk.

Isadora pulled her sister toward Max.

Rosalina had the same timid smile and thick fringed hair as Isadora, although she wore hers loose and unbraided. She grasped Max's hand and held it. "Thank you for bringing Isa to me. She told me what a good guardian you were and that you saved her more than once."

Max thought about how far he had come. There was the vast distance between here and Santa Maria, of course. But his feelings had changed, too. At first, he had thought Isadora a burden he couldn't wait to unload on the next guardian. Now he couldn't imagine being without her.

A lump formed in his throat. "I was glad . . . to be the one," he said, and meant it.

Yadra approached and explained to Isadora and Rosalina that Señorita Villa would travel with them by train. "In three days, you will be safe, somewhere far away."

"Did you hear that, Churro?" Isadora cooed softly. "We'll be safe."

Yadra shook her head. "I'm afraid Churro cannot go with you."

Isadora hugged the kitten. "He needs me."

Yadra's eyes were tender. "I am sorry. But if he is discovered, the conductor will put him off along the way and then he would be all alone in the world. That's not fair to him. And you cannot afford to draw attention to yourself or your sister."

Isadora's body crumpled.

Max cringed. He never should have allowed her to bring the kitten in the first place.

"I'll hide him. I won't let anyone see him!" Isadora's big eyes begged Max for help.

He knelt in front of her. "Why don't I take Churro home with me? Buelo and Papá would love him, and so will my aunties and Tío. You know how Churro loves Lola. We will be his family. And someday when things are safer, you could come back and visit and see how he's grown."

Tears ran down Isadora's cheeks. "You *know*

that won't happen. Nobody ever comes *back*!" She hugged Churro.

Rosalina put a hand on Isadora's shoulder. "Isa, we've come this far and don't want to get caught now, do we?"

"No . . ." she whimpered.

Max took her hand. "This is the best for Churro. It doesn't mean you don't love him." Gently, he took the kitten and handed him to Yadra. "It means you *do* love him and want him safe with people who will care for him and protect him always." As he said the words, he wondered if that was what his mother had done for him. Had she saved him from a dangerous and unpredictable life?

"You will take good care of him?" she whimpered. "And let him sleep inside?"

Max choked out his words. "Of course. I will rock him in my arms like you do, and accept his gifts of lizard tails and remember what a good mother you've been and how brave you were. He will remind me every day of you."

Her tears turned to sobs and hiccups.

Max hugged her and then leaned back. "Papá and Buelo always say, 'favor con favor se paga.' It means if you do something nice for someone, like give them your most precious kitten, then *they* should give you something in return." He slipped the compass from around his neck and put it on Isadora. "So you'll always know the way."

She closed her fingers around the small glass globe and looked up at him. "But it was your mother's. You must find her and give it back."

Max shook his head. "I can't go any farther. So I'm counting on you to keep this safe and always wear it. My mother is somewhere in Mañanaland. Maybe someday you will be a famous seamstress and own a shop and meet a brave woman with leche quemada eyes, and she'll mention that she once had a beautiful compass just like yours. Then you can tell her about me. And she'll know I am her son. And that I am safe and loved. And that I would very much like to meet her one day. Then, who knows what tomorrow might bring?"

Isadora threw her arms around Max and buried her head in his neck.

He felt her tears and whispered, "Arrorró . . . Arrorró . . ."

Yadra patted Max on the shoulder to let him know it was time.

Rosalina helped Isadora slip out of the sling and handed it to Max. She took Isadora's hand and gently guided her away into the car. Isadora pressed her face and hands on the car window, looking at Max as Señorita Villa started the motor and drove away.

Max watched the car ride the hills like a roller coaster until it disappeared. He imagined what lay beyond the horizon for Isadora and Rosalina. Mañanaland.

He hoped it all came to pass—sunshine, blue skies, flowers and fruit trees, waterfalls and rainbows. A different tomorrow, one without fear and filled with kindness, safety, and hope.

Twenty · Seven

Yadra rowed while Max sat on the bottom boards with Churro buried in the sling. The sky wavered between blue patches and menacing clouds. By midday, it rained. Yadra handed Max a hooded slicker.

"There's always a bit of melancholy when handing someone over," she said.

Max's body felt too heavy to speak.

Yadra comforted him. "You are tired from rowing and from feeling. Rest, Maximiliano. Close your eyes."

It was easy to obey. Max crossed his arms over the thwart and lay his head upon them. His lids dropped. A smothering exhaustion wrapped around him. The rhythmic click of the oarlocks and the slurp of the water sent him into a dense web at the edge of sleep.

Yadra's voice followed him. "Drag your hand in

the river. Scoop up the water but keep your fingers pressed tight like a cup. Tomorrow is there."

From the caverns of his mind, Max saw himself slowly sit up, ladle the water, and stare into the tiny lake in his palm.

It didn't feel warm and syrupy like Buelo had said. The water formed a large, solid bubble, wet and slippery, like the yolk of a fresh egg. It glowed, brightening the world around him until Max was surrounded by spaciousness. There was no horizon—no above or below. He floated within an illuminated cloud.

He could no longer see Yadra, but he could hear her humming somewhere on the periphery of his thoughts.

What worries you, Maximiliano?

His mind drifted and his voice slurred. Boys throwing rocks, people's hatred when they find out my mother was a hidden one. Being spit upon . . . treated less than human.

You will witness the best and the worst in people. Embrace the best and dismiss the worst. You are not doomed to live beneath other people's misguided notions.

Rise above their narrowness. Pity them. And create your own noble worth.

But how?

Your father's and grandfather's love is woven tightly around you and will not unravel easily. Lean on their love. Remember you don't have to struggle alone. There will always be someone who sees you and lifts you from darkness.

Will I ever meet my mother?

It's not impossible . . .

The bubble in Max's hand glimmered and trembled.

In his mind's eye, the rowboat was somewhere on the meandering river made by the serpent with the indecisive spirit. The current took him one way and then the other. He tried to reconcile the mystery of his mother, but no matter which way he turned, there were no answers or satisfaction.

Unanswered questions don't always mean a closed door. The challenge is to find an opening . . .

The uncertainty didn't feel as heavy as it once had. It felt oddly weightless and bright. The unknown was *a sliver of light streaming through a crack and beyond . . .*

to all the possibilities he could not yet see.

He might meet his mother someday.

He could make the village team.

Hopefully, he and Chuy would always be best friends.

And sooner or later Papá might shed the seriousness and worry he carried.

A strange peacefulness enveloped Max.

The bubble in his hand grew flatter, and the luster that surrounded him slowly faded.

The orb burst and, drop by drop, the water leaked through his fingers and was gone.

"Maximiliano," whispered Yadra.

Max pushed through his drowsiness and opened his eyes.

It was already late in the day. Yadra stood on the bank, holding Churro. "Maximiliano," she said again. "We are back now."

In a daze, he slowly climbed from the boat to the bank. How long had he slept?

Lola sprang to him and licked his face. The day washed a feeling of urgency over him. "I . . . I have to get home."

Yadra looked at the sky and nodded. "The rain has stopped and there are a few hours of light left. If you leave soon, you can make it to one of the resting places. Come. You'll have to exit the way you came. Find your backpack and I'll gather some provisions for you and the animals." She waved him into the cavern.

As Max watched Yadra stuff his backpack with a blanket and food, his heart filled with gratitude, not only for what she'd done to help Rosalina and Isadora, but for her kindness to Max, too. He wasn't sure how, but talking to her had lightened his spirit. Buelo had been right about her great wisdom and mesmerizing aura.

As he stood beneath the bridge, ready to set out for home, he hugged her. "Thank you, Yadra. For everything. I hope we meet again."

"We will," she said, patting him on the back. "Sooner or later, there will be someone who needs a guardian. We will have many more tomorrows. Of that I am certain." She held him at arm's length and winked. "Did I mention that I love visitors?"

Max laughed. "Yes, you did. And dogs and cats, too."

Twenty · Eight

Max set out, never questioning that the path he was on was leading to a place he wanted to go.

He retraced the same route, this time walking all the way across the Bridge of a Thousand Mallards. Churro was snug against his chest in the sling, and Lola sensed they were headed home. She pulled on the leash, and Max let himself be led.

Yadra had warned him to stay hidden as much as possible. If anyone questioned him about the girl with a price on her head, he was to say she'd run away.

That first night, after he spread out the blanket, Churro walked all around it, sniffing and meowing. "I know," said Max. "I miss her, too." He pulled a sandwich from his backpack and fed every other pinch to Churro or Lola. Then he put Churro on his chest, scooted closer to Lola, and pulled a blanket over the three of them. He slept lightly, woke early, and the next day walked until almost dark.

On the morning of the third day, he sat on the bank of the river, studying the map while Lola and Churro played nearby. He was covering ground quickly. If he kept going, he might make it home by evening.

What would Papá say when he saw him? Would he be angry that Max had disobeyed him? Or would he be proud of what Max had done, as Yadra had said?

As he continued walking the river's path, the warm summer air enveloped him. The sunlight began to fade. He rounded a bend, and his breath caught. There, on a boulder only a few feet away, sat the peregrine!

Lola barked, sending the falcon into the sky before she settled in a tree farther downriver. When Max caught up to her, she lifted and circled to another tree. Each time Max thought she had flown away for good, she reappeared.

"Pilgrim bird, whose spirit do you carry beneath your wings?" He thought of Isadora. Was she sending

Max a message that she was safe? Or was it his mother's spirit watching over him and guiding him home?

By the time Max reached the citrus orchards and grape fields on the outskirts of Santa Maria, it was dusk. The peregrine careened and dived above him, then headed straight for the horizon, where the merlons and crenels of La Reina Gigante peeked above the treetops and beckoned.

Max startled as a shadow moved toward him. Lola raised her head and growled. Max pulled her toward him and crouched behind a boulder, his heart pounding.

Footsteps thudded closer. Lola leaped forward, barking. She was straining so hard on the leash, he had to let go.

"Max?"

Relief washed over him.

"Papá?"

Papá ran toward him and Max fell into his arms. Lola yelped and ran circles around them.

Papá held him at arm's length. His eyes were

dark, worried hollows. "I arrived home this afternoon and set out immediately. Are you okay?"

"I'm fine," Max said, and then his words spilled. "I'm sorry, Papá. I shouldn't have gone to the ruins alone, or disobeyed Buelo, or lied to Father Romero. Everyone was probably worried. I thought I could find her and—"

"Slow down," said Papá. "Start from the beginning. Buelo said you took someone to the secret bridge . . . ?"

Max nodded and told Papá all about Isadora and how she was safe with her sister now.

Papá patted him on the back and shook his head as if he couldn't believe what he was hearing. "Max . . . why would you volunteer to do something so dangerous?"

"It didn't seem dangerous in the beginning. But then . . ."

Papá nodded. "A young girl's life was at stake. And yours was, too. It must have been scary."

"Yes, Papá," Max said, feeling the seriousness of

what he'd done. "But I thought if I went, I could find my mother . . . and she'd want to come home . . . and you could believe in happy endings again . . . and you would see that I can do things . . . that I'm capable."

Papá shook his head. "Oh, Max, I *do* believe in happy endings because you are back safe and sound. I could never bear to lose you." He pulled Max to his chest and held him for a long time.

When he finally let go, Max said, "I have so many questions. And you promised you'd tell me everything when you returned."

Papá nodded solemnly. He led Max along the riverbank, and they slowly walked toward home hand-in-hand. "I should have told you before. But I wanted to protect you as long as I could. You see, your mother—"

"Was a hidden one. I know, Papá. I found the stone rubbing in your papers and went to the tower and figured it out. I'm sorry I snooped and disobeyed you, but I needed to know more about her, and me."

"I'm sorry it came to that." Papa sighed. "I don't know where to start."

"Start at the beginning," said Max.

Papá squeezed his hand. "I was home between seasons on the national team when a guardian arrived at the cottage. He had just escorted a group of women, including your mother, to the tower. As quickly as we could, Buelo, Tío, Mariana, Amelia, and I helped move the women a few at a time to the next safe place. Except your mother. She had fallen and sprained her ankle. We couldn't bring her to the village because someone might report her or us. We all agreed that she should hide in the tower until she was strong enough to travel. In the meantime, Buelo made her a crutch so she could move around the ruins."

"She must have been scared and lonely at the tower by herself."

"I came every day. Your aunties, and Buelo or Tío often brought food and supplies." Papá smiled. "Even in those conditions, she was always humming or singing. I would walk through the clearing and before I even caught sight of her, I'd hear that beautiful voice. She sang while washing, picking berries, or sitting in the sun and mending. She was so happy to be *anywhere* besides Abismo and so grateful for the smallest kindness."

"What happened to her in Abismo?" asked Max.

Papá sighed. "She wouldn't say. She never talked about her life before."

Max thought about Isadora and Rosalina, and the awful man they had finally escaped. Had something similar happened to his mother?

"My heart broke just knowing she'd come from such horrible circumstances. I was very young and I wanted to save her. I asked her to marry me. I thought I was doing such a good thing and that it was the answer to all her problems. Anyway, she said yes and—"

"You got married at Our Lady of Sorrows?" asked Max.

Papá shook his head. "You've heard how

villagers talk about people from Abismo. We had to keep our relationship secret, at least in the beginning. And I couldn't admit to being a guardian."

"Then how—?"

"Buelo was asked to build a bridge in San Clemente that would take over a year to complete. I took the job instead and secretly brought her with me. While we were gone, Buelo told people that I'd met someone there, married, and was going to be a father. After the bridge was finished, you were born and we moved back to Santa Maria and lived in an apartment in the village. As far as anyone knew, or knows even now, your mother was from San Clemente."

"Is that why you quit fútbol?"

"In part, yes. But there were other reasons, too. My own mother had died a few years earlier, and Buelo was struggling with the business. He needed me. You and your mother needed me. It was a difficult choice, but I don't regret it."

Ortiz had mocked, *Some love story, huh?* But it

was romantic to Max, like a fairy tale. "Then why did she leave?"

Papá shook his head. "We thought she was happy. We were a family, doing all the things people who love one another do. Sunday dinners with the family. Picnics at the river. All of us reveling in the delight a baby brings. And then . . ."

"What happened?"

"I needed to repair a bridge in a remote area. While I was gone, a guardian brought two young women to the tower. For the few nights they were there, your mother helped them. Then one morning she brought you to Buelo's and asked if he could watch you. She gave some excuse about errands and said she'd be back later in the day. But instead, she went to the ruins and escorted the two women to the next safe place and . . . never returned."

"How did she know the way?"

"She'd heard us all talk about the route and the secret bridge enough times. She'd seen the map . . . When she didn't return, Buelo went to the apartment and found that everything had been left in perfect order. She had cleaned, done the laundry, stocked the cupboards, and had sewn clothes for you in different sizes. They were all laid out in neat stacks on the table. She must have been working on them for months. Maybe it was in anticipation that she might someday have to leave suddenly. Or maybe she had been planning to leave and had been waiting for just the right moment. She took all of her things, every photograph she was in, and any paper with her name on it. I suppose so there was no trace left of her."

"Yadra said the fear of being discovered runs very deep."

"She's right," said Papá. "Your mother did leave a note . . ."

"I saw it." Sadness and hurt squeezed Max all over again. "So all that time you thought we were a happy family, she was planning to leave?"

Papá put his arm around Max. "I don't know. I know she loved us. I suspect someone found out she was a hidden one and confronted her. Or maybe she was afraid that someone from her past life would eventually catch up to her, and if she was caught, we would all be in danger. I even wondered if the two women she helped had brought some threatening news from Abismo. I just don't know." He blew out a long breath.

"Why didn't she take me with her?"

"It would have been too risky to travel with a baby. Here with us, you had a safe and loving home, a community. Her future and safety were unknown. And I am so thankful she didn't take you. I cannot imagine my life without you." Papá pulled him closer. "I would have been heartbroken to lose my boy. You gave me a reason to get on with my life. Over time, I had to start accepting that she was gone."

Max couldn't picture his life without Papá either. "But you said you've never stopped looking for her? Wasn't it to convince her to come home?"

"No, Max. At that point I knew we wouldn't be together again. At first, I searched so I might convince her to give me the papers she took. But as the years passed, I continued to search—through every crowd, every marketplace, every large gathering—to make sure she, or someone she sent, didn't show up and try to take you."

"Could that happen?" asked Max.

"When you were younger, yes. She had all the documents to prove you were her son, and I had none. I admit, the fear of you being kidnapped has caused me—and all of us—a lot of anxiety over the years. That's why Buelo and I, and Tío and your aunties, never let you out of our sight. But even now, that slim fear that it could still happen haunts me."

Max stopped walking. Everything finally made sense, and he felt his eyes fill with tears for all that Papá had been carrying. "Papá, you don't have to worry anymore. And you don't have to struggle alone. No matter what happens, I would always find my way home to you. But I . . . I need you to see that I'm older now, and growing up."

Papá's eyes glistened in the twilight. He pulled

out his handkerchief and dabbed them. "I do see it, son. I'm sorry it has taken me so long."

"And, Papá, I *like* talking about my mother. Even if I never meet her, I want to know about her. What if she had taken me and never told me anything about you? My life would have been so empty not knowing about you and Buelo and Tío and my aunties and my life in Santa Maria."

"I only meant to protect you. I didn't want your life to be filled with sad illusions and false hope, or dreams that would never come true."

"I like illusions and hope and dreams, whether they come true or not." Max stood taller. "I know you probably don't believe me, but I went on a journey with Yadra. I held tomorrow in the palm of my hand." He braced himself for Papá's doubt.

But Papá just pulled Max close and rested his cheek against Max's forehead. "I never told you," he whispered. "I once held tomorrow in my hands, too."

Max couldn't believe it. "Papá! When?"

"The day you were born."

Max smiled. "And was the path you were on leading to the place you wanted to go?"

"Of course," said Papá. "It still is."

They rocked back and forth until Lola tried to squeeze into the embrace and Churro squirmed.

"What is this?" asked Papá, patting Max's chest.

He carefully lifted the sleeping kitten out of the sling and handed him to Papá. "Papá, meet Churro, the newest member of our family."

As they walked, Papa cradled the kitten in one arm and kept Max close with the other.

When all of La Reina Gigante came into view, Max knew they were almost home. As the light waned and the world grew dim, she kept watch over them.

"Papá, what happened in San Clemente?"

"I followed Tío's recommendation and contacted everyone I could think of who knew you as a baby. I talked to people here in Santa Maria, and I even knocked on the door of old neighbors in San

Clemente and found the doctor who delivered you. They all sent letters."

"And Father Romero?"

"Yes, him too. If the application is approved, the official documents will be mailed. But will it be in time for fútbol registration? I will be honest, I am not sure. With any luck . . ."

"Papá! Did you say with any *luck*?" Max grinned.

Papá laughed out loud. "I think I did."

Max knew the papers might arrive in time or they might not.

He took Papá's hand and whispered, "Solo mañana sabe. But in my mind, I am hoping for good luck, too."

Twenty · Nine

The last game of the season was against Santa Inés in their stadium for the regional championship.

Nearly all of Santa Maria turned out for it, taking buses and piling into cars and trucks. Even Max's aunties and Miss Domínguez took the bus with Buelo and Tío.

Papá and Max rode with the team.

There hadn't been any more talk about Papá being a criminal. Tío had put an end to all the rumors. No one knew about Max's mother being a hidden one either, at least for now. But if it was discovered, Max was prepared to tell anyone who she really was—a brave and selfless hero who wanted to protect her family and to live life without fear.

Max knew who he was, too—someone who was true of heart and proud of the legacy into which he'd been born.

He came from a long line of stonemasons who

built bridges that never collapsed and allowed one side of the river to hold hands with the other.

Fútbol was in his blood—the talent hadn't skipped him—and with hard work and practice, he had made the village team and might one day make the national team.

He was a Guardian of the Hidden Ones.

Max lined up on the field with his teammates in their green-and-white uniforms. The soft, snug leather of his now well-loved Volantes hugged his feet. Papá had bought them in San Clemente. Max had earned them after working all summer as his apprentice.

He didn't use them to spring from one side of the goal posts to the other, though. Ortiz played goalie. He'd done well at the summer clinic and honed his skills. He was the best choice. Chuy was center back, Gui a midfielder, and Max played forward.

The coach, Héctor Cruz, paid attention to him, saying he hadn't seen such fast feet in a long time.

When he found out that Papá had once played professional, he asked him to help with the team. Even Buelo sometimes came out to watch their practices and to show all the players the photo of him and Nandito.

Héctor Cruz had high hopes for this team.

The stadium was full and the crowd wild. With little time on the clock, the score was tied. The fans swayed and sang, "Santa Mar-EEE-ah. Santa Mar-EEE-ah."

An opponent dribbled toward Max. He was big, like a mountain moving in his direction. But Max attacked and stole the ball, then kicked it back to Gui. He ran toward the goal and pushed around a player to get open. Gui passed the ball to him. Max trapped it and dribbled around a defender. When he saw an opening, he kicked the ball and scored!

The whistle screamed.

They'd won! The cheering, like thunder, filled the stadium. Max raised his arms and ran in a circle.

Papá rushed to him from the sidelines and lifted him off the ground in a giant hug. Then, with their arms around each other, they looked toward the stands. Papá pointed to a section, and Max spotted Buelo, Tío, his aunties, and Miss Domínguez. They waved and cheered madly.

Just as he did at the end of every game, he scanned the stadium of people. He knew that neither one of them was likely there, but just in case the impossible became possible, he waved his arm in a wide arc, back and forth.

Chuy flung himself at Max. "Hermano, we did it! We're champions!"

His teammates surrounded him. In a giant huddle, the team began to chant, "CÓR-doe-bah! CÓR-doe-bah! CÓR-doe-bah!"

Max felt like he could fly.

Thirty

Saturday night during a windstorm, Buelo made himself comfortable with a cup of coffee in his chair that sagged in all the right places. Max claimed one corner of the sofa and Papá the other. Lola lay on the tiles in front of the fireplace. Churro batted at the brooms of rosemary in the firebox.

"Maximiliano, it is your turn to tell," said Buelo. "I told last week."

Max held up a finger. "Remind me, how do I begin?"

Buelo beamed. "Once upon a time . . ."

Max cleared his throat. "Once upon a time, there was a princess from a faraway land who did not want to marry the man her parents chose for her. They did not *see* her or notice she had a mind of her own. Besides, the man . . ."

". . . was mean and smelly," said Buelo.

"And liked to eat toads for dinner," said Papá.

"Exactly," said Max.

"So she ran away to a grand palace in the next kingdom and hid in a deserted tower. She didn't know it, but a dragon owned the palace grounds. At first, when the dragon discovered the princess, he was nice and friendly and he said she could live there, too. Why not?"

"The more the merrier," said Papá.

Max laughed. "I am telling the story! The dragon became more and more protective of the princess, barely allowing her out of his sight. He began to think that she was his possession.

"One day, when she was doing laundry at the river, she met a man from the local village and over time, they fell in love and secretly married. But when the dragon discovered the news, he became so angry and jealous, he stomped around the palace and made the earth shake. The walls fell down and the floors crumbled."

"He went on a rampage," Papá added.

Max nodded. "Only the tower remained. The

princess and her husband ran away. Months later, they had a baby.

"The dragon grew jealous and more furious every day," Max continued. "One night, the dragon kidnapped the princess, took her away from her husband and baby, and brought her back to the tower. With magic, the dragon turned her into a peregrine falcon and caged her in the domed tower room. But one day, a storm tore the tiles off the roof and the peregrine princess escaped. Finally free, she flew away to live among other birds. She nests high on a hilltop, where she still lives today."

"I hope that is not the end," said Buelo.

"No," said Max. "Sometimes she soars over the small village where she once lived with her husband and baby, hoping to see them from the sky. And when she does, she swoops as close as she dares, and sings, '*Arrorró, mi niño. Arrorró, mi sol. Arrorró, pedazo de mi corazón.*'"

Outside, the wind whistled, but inside the room was quiet. Max's words settled around them like downy feathers drifting to the floor.

Papá whispered, "Bravo."

Buelo wiped tears from his eyes. "One of your best."

Papá helped Max up, hugged him, and said, "Off to bed now. I'm going out for a while."

"Tell Miss Domínguez the story," said Max.

Papá smiled. "I will."

Before he went to sleep, Max stood at his window and looked at La Reina Gigante. He and Papá had been there recently to collect stones. The peregrine had long ago left the nest, until next spring. Max had gone inside the tower, and as promised, he finished carving Isadora's name on the stone next to her sister's, to show she had made it that far.

He gazed up at the tower now and whispered, "La Reina, do you believe in happy endings?"

The moon shone on her face. Leaves swirled through the air. Distant clouds raced behind her. Within the night's frenzy, her crown seemed to bob back and forth.

And Max had his answer.

Acknowledgments

A book has many guardians.

I am grateful first and always to my editor, Tracy Mack, who shepherded this book through my many tangents and meanderings. The story and I would be lost and mired if it weren't for her thoughtful and unfailing direction.

Heartfelt appreciation to those who held *Mañanaland*'s hand along the way: assistant editor Benjamin Gartenberg, art director Marijka Kostiw, copy editor Kerianne Steinberg, production editor Melissa Schirmer, and everyone in publicity and marketing—especially Lizette Serrano, Rachel Feld, Lauren Donovan, Elisabeth Ferrari, Emily Heddleson, and Erin Berger. And to Paola Escobar for her stunning art, un mil gracias!

Early readers, my cultural caretakers, gave me valuable advice. Thank you to researcher Jerusha Saldaña Yáñez; Laura Carmen Arena, former Assistant Director for Multicultural Affairs at the Harvard Graduate School of Education; and Andres Aranda.

I am forever indebted to my extended Scholastic family for their continued support and enthusiasm. Special thanks to the entire trade and library marketing and sales teams and to the booksellers, librarians, and educators who introduce my books to readers.

The text of this book is set in 12 point Athelas Regular, designed by

Veronika Burian and José Scaglione in 2008, and inspired

by British fine book printing.

The display font is set in Swingdancer, and was designed by

Chank Diesel in 2006. Diesel's fonts were featured in the

Smithsonian's Cooper-Hewitt National Design Museum as

"important examples of contemporary typography."

The wraparound jacket illustration was

created digitally by Paola Escobar.

The book was printed on Norbrite Offset and

bound at LSC Communications.

Production was overseen by Melissa Schirmer.

Manufacturing was supervised by Irene Chan.

The book was designed by Marijka Kostiw

and edited by Tracy Mack.